SKULLY

JAMES GHOLSON JR.

outskirts
press

Skully
All Rights Reserved.
Copyright © 2018 James Gholson, Jr.
v3.0

This is a work of fiction. The events and characters described herein are imaginary and are not intended to refer to specific places or living persons. The opinions expressed in this manuscript are solely the opinions of the author and do not represent the opinions or thoughts of the publisher. The author has represented and warranted full ownership and/or legal right to publish all the materials in this book.

This book may not be reproduced, transmitted, or stored in whole or in part by any means, including graphic, electronic, or mechanical without the express written consent of the publisher except in the case of brief quotations embodied in critical articles and reviews.

Outskirts Press, Inc.
http://www.outskirtspress.com

ISBN: 978-1-4787-9309-0

Library of Congress Control Number: 2018901054

Cover Image by Kyle Neblett

Outskirts Press and the "OP" logo are trademarks belonging to Outskirts Press, Inc.

PRINTED IN THE UNITED STATES OF AMERICA

I

They came to this place, up long slopes from the landing dock, to join the Tennessee 13th Cavalry. They hailed from all parts of the country—North Carolina, Virginia, South Carolina, Mississippi, and Tennessee. The songs they sang fueled both work and prayer; the boots they wore pinched their toes. They came to this place as freedom fighters for family members, for liberty, and for the Union. The muskets they'd been issued came *before* education, as did the uniforms that clothed their backs. They'd been sparked by calls for volunteers by Frederick Douglass, prodded by advancing Union armies and emboldened with random opportunities for escape from slavery. Heartened by the Emancipation Proclamation, they bolted to Union lines, many accompanied by their children, wives, and loved ones, known worldwide as refugees, but here, called *contraband*. Emboldened by victories in the

JAMES GHOLSON, JR.

West, they scurried to Union outposts and fortresses—Negley, Pickering, Corinth—to claim manhood, though many had yet to learn to read and write.

"Dese here boots be mighty tight," said one.

"Ain't nuthin," said another. "Be lak a pincer movement, only dey be surroundin' yo' feets, 'stead of your butt! Ain't nowheres near as tight as massa's chains; jus' make sure you don' step on non a dem mule biscuits up yonder. Stank up yer boots fur days." The discovery of nests of cottonmouth snakes in the vicinity caused the men to sleep in their boots during the night. "Dey kin crawl up 'side your boots, strike 'em real good, your feet. Poison you right in dere in ya sleep."

"Yep, better blisters den dying from poison. Tell me Johnnies lak dem pincer movements," said another.

One of the officers, impressed with the efficiency of their drill, spoke to them with a respect of tone they cherished. "And pincer movements can happen fast. You boys did nice work today; I appreciate your hard work. Taps is sounding soon, so sleep well." He said nothing of the gossip regarding secesh in the vicinity, of Union City or Paducah. He also said nothing of Ben's observation, "We can't get the cannon sufficiently depressed to hit low-lying objects."

"Yessir," they answered in scattered unison as

they spied the officer passing, tiptoeing through damp ground on the way to his cabin. Beneath a thin tin plate, they jiggled and stoked the lowermost twigs to stimulate a campfire. One or two of them snuggled under individual raingear as a light drizzle persisted. They knew they were becoming a team. They could feel military magic transfer from theory to muscle through practice; now the muscle-memory slipped into their bones: *bone-memory.* "Ah be glad to have dis here musket, be even gladder if'n Ah could read and write. Missin' ma kinfolk sumpthin' terr'ble. Betcha dem Rebs git here 'fore week's end," said Dan.

Their practice with long-arms had gone well too, not to mention the teamwork necessary for serving—loading and firing—cannons. Many had enlisted at Corinth and the two companies of USCT (United States Colored Troops)—the Second Light and the Sixth Heavy—had been at the fort less than two weeks. They prayed, joked, and teased one another while speculating on their new condition: *freedom.* In the distance, they heard colleagues and comrades singing spirituals and marching songs as day darkened into night. They had climbed "Jacob's Ladder" and reached Canaan—the Promised Land—and they were soldiers and free. "Take you up on dat bet; pitch in a dollar all around for de pot!" said Elias.

"Whose got fixin's?" asked Sandy, smiling as he

posed the question, smiling as he examined faces for age and likelihood. He sat wide-legged, close to the fizzle and pop of blackened logs. He'd overheard their white counterparts refer to black Unionists as smoked-Yankees, galvanized-Yankees, mokes, and, of course, niggers. "Extra dollar for namin' time of day and callin' who wins, who loses—us or de Rebs. Remember now, Rebs don' take no black prisoners of war—dey ain't got time to 'scort you back to de plantation!" They laughed from the belly, deep and husky.

The place sloped into the river in multiple guises; some slopes were almost ninety degrees into the water, others gentler, like the one into the landing dock. All slopes ended in the Mississippi. To this small garrison, their presence added heavy and light artillery, dutifully hefted up these same slopes.

The boy amongst them said, "Ah laked dat roar when you make dat cannon speak. The arc you take on dose shells puts a powerful skeer on de crows but nevah striked nuthin' up close or down low. Always fallin' beyond that snake-filled gully. Ah be right glad to have dis here musket close, be even gladder if Ah had a revolver. Missin' ma kinfolk sumthin' terr'ble too. Kin you read, write a letter?" As the boy spoke, he yanked up britches a size too large.

Ben studied the boy suspecting he had a warrior's eye for defense, knowing he had a remarkable shooter's eye. Ben knew you could get bent backward, feel blisters like buckshot burning your britches, if you got the lanyard tangled trying to get the cannon to "speak," as the boy put it. "A bit," he said.

Sandy added, "Heard they call white folks from 'round dese here parts home-grown Yankees—Lordy, what will dey think up next? Crackers is a mess." Shadows of the men flickered against the tents close by and the trees further beyond.

The younger man, actually a boy in uniform, handed Sandy a cigarette already rolled. "Ah come prepared," he said.

Dan looked at him and shook his head. "A li'l wh-upsnapper lak you—would nevah knowed it, but Ah gotta admit, you sure kin shoot, boy, sure kin. Why, I bet ain't nobody 'round dese here parts dun' thought you evah gots your pecker wet." The boy laughed but said nothing. "Dat's the surefire truth, though, son, you kin sure shoot!"

"Yeah, but I need me a revolver," said the boy. "Heard dat all Forrest's men carry revolvers 'steada sabers—mainly 'cause sabers be both bulky and noisy."

"How long you been smokin', boy?" said Elias.

"Longer 'n you, big brother; ain't gon' say what else," and a long, winding grin broke out on his lips, crawled up to his cheek, and danced to his eyes and forehead. Illuminated by the campfire, his lips blossomed, his cheeks glowed rosy, his eyes sparkled, and his forehead bobbed and weaved. Ha-ha's from his laughter echoed about the nearby ravines and chattered down crooked Mississippi banks. His teeth, brightened by the glow, threw splinters of red and white that gleamed on toothy enamel. Once recovered, the boy added, "I 'magine the slope on de north-most part of dis place is 'bout most seventy degrees, whereby southwards—on de road we come up—twenty-five or thirty, four-hundred or four-fifty feet, here to down yonder."

"You be issue free?" said Ben.

"Dat be good quesshun—ain't speakin' to it," said the boy. "Ah dun' heard dat ole Forrest's men be considered infantry aboard horseback. Yessir, dun' shore heard dat comin' straight from de occifer's mouth. Speedy movement on horseback, accurate firing on foot."

"Officer's mouth, son—say it slow like, off-fice-sir—den they respond correct."

"Kin sure do dat—when dose stanky feet a yourn's gets aired out."

Laughter got passed out all around, like drinks at a bar.

A small cache of brown-skinned men looked to a sergeant to lead them in a group prayer. The white men of the 13th Cavalry sang verses ending with,

"We're marching south to Canaan, to battle for the Lord." Not far away, a sergeant led blacks of a small splinter group in "Jacob's Ladder . . . soldiers of the cross."

"Each man gets to the Lord in his own way," said Elias, adding, "You mighty quiet, Ben—what's got you thinkin' so much?" Ben Robinson liked to throw out problems to a group; sometimes it helped him to come up with answers, prodded him toward fresh options.

"Look," Ben said, "I gots two problems; one, if the secesh get down in those ravines, I can't lower the cannons enough to aim at 'em—parapets too wide; two, boy here is right about dose ravines and revolvers—and guess what?—If sharpshooters get up on them knolls out yonder, we be in a world of hurt, plus we ain't had the first evacuation drill." He punched at the twitch in his thigh.

"The 13th already been out here for a while. Seems like they woulda cleant dis place up a bit and built abatis—logs everywhere," said the boy, "and how many dollars be in dat pot when we fellaship wid dem Rebs?"

"Thought about that and 'spose to get some action on it soon, whenever that be," said Elias, "plus we gots to cut down some trees, build abatis, angle dem cannon ports."

"Meanin' *we* gets to do it," said Sandy.

Rain drizzled less hard now on the thin tin which shielded the fire from extinction. Nearby, they could hear the bugler doing his warm-up routine: buzzing on the mouthpiece. Now and then the firewood popped, crackling against the fall of casual raindrops. "But you know—sure you know this already—there are some folk, black folk, dat are believin' on the Rebels. Now how you figure on dat?" said Dan.

"Dun' heard dat one too; takin' their chances on de Confederates winnin'. Old Tubman dun' said already, 'Saved a thousand slaves to freedom and coulda saved a thousand mo', if'n dey knew dey were slaves.' I figure many waited to see which way fortunes break; smart really. Fortunes break at different times for different folk; miss some altogether. Don' git no mo' confusin' den dat. Gonna turn in. Sleep tight; dey gon' blow taps any minute," said Ben. He tugged at his rain slicker, tightening it around his chest, massaged his nervous, twitching thigh, and headed for his tent. For some strange reason, his palms felt sweaty. *Is there reason to be nervous?* he wondered and fell asleep before the notes of taps came to an end.

II

Two days ago I was at an estate sale for a friend of mine named Jesse who, in actuality, was a friend of my dad's and a man who played a big part in my life. It was an interesting estate sale, full of antique furniture, a grand variety of objects d'art and books galore. For the curious they included a variety of titles—many of which I'd never heard of—and which had been read with intensity. By that, I mean they'd been read repeatedly, with questions in the margins, selected portions underlined and marked with emoticons in spots, and written questions all over the place. There were even pages in manuscript; handwritten pages of a full chapter—the preceding chapter which I just read out loud—fell out of the book as I picked it up. The book was about a group of scouts, Harvey's scouts, who operated in the western theater of the Civil War. The manuscript that fell out of the book seemed written in the hand of this man

JAMES GHOLSON, JR.

Jesse who, when I was a boy, would give me a brand-new, bright silver dollar on Sundays after church, as he and my dad talked politics. I dusted the cover of the book and clutched it, and the hand-written pages, to my side while I browsed titles of other books unfamiliar to me: Dubois's *Black Reconstruction*, 1935, Cruse's *Crisis of the Negro Intellectual*, 1967, G. W. William's *History of the Negro Troops in the War of the Rebellion*, 1887, Morrison's *Beloved*, 1987, and a slew of maps of the Washington, D. C., metropolitan area. I had known Jesse since being a kid, but had little knowledge of his intellectual life and the stuff he read or talked about. The only book in his collection that I knew was by Toni Morrison.

I bought the unfamiliar ones for pennies, feeling my pulse perk, my step gain a bit of pluck and a surge of anticipation electrify my curiosity. The chapter imagined a fight, anticipated the imagined with curiosity, and initiated a journey, an offshoot, if you will, that played a mysterious part in my career journey. I wondered where to place that first chapter in the scheme of these pages and decided to put it at the beginning . . . because it captures—illustrates—a sense of trepidation; it *seizes* my own sense of emotional apprehension and suspense as these men prepare to "fellaship" with fate.

My name is Caleb, and I am a student at Harrison

University majoring in architecture. This is my fourth year; I have one more to go. I live on two hills: one where I attend school, the other where I fill in on occasion as a waiter, close to Capitol Hill. And, no, I am not preparing for war; in fact, my apprehension comes from preparing to enter the architectural profession and learning the ropes of interviews and employment seeking.

"The Hill" is the name of the restaurant, and on the day of my appointment for employment, the owner was present. "I like to talk with prospective hires . . . chat with them a bit on their goals, what they are up to, where they come from," he said. I explained to him that I was close to finishing my degree program at Harrison and have to earn extra money to defray school costs. "I have an academic scholarship and maintain a solid average," I said. Luckily, he didn't ask me what my numerical average was.

Even though I possessed talent, some of my professors thought my work overly pedestrian, uninspired. In truth, I purposefully underachieved so as not to inspire either jealousy or incur rancor from my peers. I was surprised at what I had accomplished so far, and bemused by my modest speed in pursuit of my architectural degree. My heart for the art ran at one hundred and twenty miles per hour; my study skills cruised at seventy-eight. Is there a frightening hole in my psychological stamina with regard to my talent? When do I energize my ability to address, rectify, and challenge this? Some suggested more curiosity, more aggressiveness—even hypnosis—would help. I knew, deep down, that I needed a mentor—dead or alive—as my personal guide. Someone professional, an African American who had met the challenge of meshing the great art of the West—its discipline, glory, craft, and philosophies—with the African American experience.

"I have a 'B+' average," I said, blurting.

"You went to high school in the area?" he asked.

"Oh yeah—out at Fairmont Heights."

"The Heights—man, y'all got a fabulous rep in basketball. I remember when the Heights was mighty. Been awhile, though. I remember seeing 'Ducie Smith' back in the day," the owner said. I enjoyed the bartending and the spirited camaraderie around the place. I just wasn't called in that often, but the little bit of money helped with odds and ends. I do remember one weekend night when a group came in wearing Confederate uniforms. Most of them wore kepis—old Civil War caps—like the ones familiar during that period. All of them were sweaty wearing that stuff, even though it wasn't summertime-warm yet.

"Beers all around," said one of them, "whatever you have on tap."

"Beers all around coming up," I repeated. I had just finished cleaning things up a little—rearranging chairs, wiping tables, sweeping the floors, and cleaning my hands. From their conversation, I gathered that they were from various parts of the Old Dominion state. I took in the order in parcels and got them all set up in three trips. "My name is Caleb; I'll be your server. Anything else I can get you?" The guzzle was on, and I heard nothing. "Holler if you need me," I said.

When I got back to my position behind the bar, I heard the word "Garçon" ring out. I anchored my instincts, went to the table, presented a smile, and said, "What do you need, fellas?" Snickers rolled from two of the younger ones.

"Can't drink beer without peanuts; how about a bucket?"

"No problem—coming right up," I said.

Luckily, Jeff, one of the bouncers, was close by. I fish-eyed him and watched as he went to the table and reminded them that, "His name is Caleb, y'all. That Gen'ral Lee was a real respectful type." I winked at him, remembering that the manager had cautioned me: "Negative experiences do happen. Sometimes it's best just to take the money and run."

I kept my smile on, delivered the peanuts, and worked on the balance of chairs and tables. Boss

JAMES GHOLSON, JR.

could come in anytime. To my great surprise, a couple of those fellas got up and started dancing Irish reels to sung strains of "Dixie." I tracked Jeff down at the door as he ushered in a rather large group of army soldiers, still in uniform, from Fort McNair. He placed them fairly near my Dixiecrats and everything seemed to calm down a good bit after that. The soldiers wanted beer too, and I brought an extra bucket for Lee's protégées and a new one for the soldiers. I must confess that I do often wonder, with all that access to traveling and great cultural access—to art, music, books, history—in Washington, D.C. (no slave or black codes, no Jim Crow), why one sees "wild and woolly" from young white men. But then, you see that behavior more and more these days from young black men too.

"Twinkle-toes" had stopped and I didn't hear "Garçon" another time that whole evening. Twenty minutes or so after the soldiers came in, Jeff sat down a group of cadets from Harrison U. Apparently, they were having a fencing contest on campus, and we chatted a bit. They invited me to the competition, and then passed out invites to the Rebs and the army soldiers. I never found out how that went over. But it was followed by the damnedest thing. The guys from Harrison started singing a marching song. I saved one of the lyrics left behind on a piece of paper.

SKULLY

These are the swarthy bondsmen,
The iron-skinned brigade,
They pile up freedom's breastworks,
They'll scoop out rebels' graves,
Then who will be their owner
And march them off for slaves?

I made a good chunk of change that night and made a solemn prayer to my dad who had passed two years before from a stroke. His passing had devastated my mom, particularly since it was so unexpected. That was two years of history now, and I was in my fourth year of a five-year program. I'd promised Daddy I would finish my degree.

III

Tension is an essential element in the chemistry of the black experience; probably to any human experience. At "The Hill" restaurant, there was a swinging door to the kitchen; timed effectively, I could make it through that door; timed improperly, that door could send me flying backward in the direction of approach. That swinging door also swung within my brain as a psychic posture, a mental tension of stop or go, acceptance or repudiation. *Did I walk on a tripwire?* I could see daylight, and run for it, as Lombardi would say, or be repudiated in a stunning tackle. Timing was the key ingredient allowing or denying success.

I wanted success, to gain access to fulfillment of my individual journey into full exploration of human potential, of *my* potential. The black middle class—those who read and write—are perennially subjected to *achievement-disbelief* by some whites and *achievement-jealousy* by some blacks. This awareness, called a double-consciousness by some, creates a push and pull, a swing and sway, a living dialectic, in which I vacillated. I felt buoyed on a swing with limited control of my future, further complicated by a tight financial condition. I knew my study was coming to an end, and then competition for life would become even more real: food-on-the-table real. Even though I loved architectural design and had worked for a dollar here and there, I wasn't sure I could bring the full focus of my imagination into my work. *Am I afraid to try, to fail?* I asked myself. Dean Davenport, dean of the architecture school, had put his finger on the pulse of my doughnut hole: a prevailing lack of confidence and grit, necessary to revise and energize my imagination. I felt a frozen feeling embrace me. Often, I searched out someone close, usually older, about their life experiences, about the answers—both true and false—they found along the way.

The recent summons I'd received from Davenport had provoked my anxieties. *Can I really compete, really sprint to win?* I wondered, stalemated in chronic stupor. Heck, I had pursued my academics in a sluggish trot, not even a slow trot, mainly to minimize social target practice from anybody. "At some point before graduation, you might need to ratchet your attitude up a notch," was said by one professor. The first person I wanted to check in with was Jesse, my dad's old buddy. For some unknown reason, I remembered "Slow Trot," the moniker Jesse had used to tease Daddy about his favorite general, George Henry Thomas. Jesse had retired and was now church warden at New Canaan Baptist Church, just off the H Street corridor, on Sixth Northeast.

Gawking at the church as Jesse approached, I'd already spent four or five minutes studying the statuesque architecture of the place; the now sooty Ashlar bricks, the stained-glass windows, and the wrought-iron fence that surrounded the place.

"Well, if it ain't young Caleb! Boy, it sure is good to see you, li'l brother," and he gave me a double brohug. "You ain't nowhere near as regular 'round this place as you were when your dad was livin'," said Jesse. The bricks were much darker than I remembered as a child.

"Hi, Jesse," I said, "long time no see, man. Great to see you. Church looks good, maybe kinda sooty from all that subway construction. How have you been?"

"Good, Caleb, good—maybe a little wobbly 'bout the knees—but that's the price of living these days."

The church had been standing since the late eighteen hundreds, a handsome reminder of D.C. architecture at that time. We hung about the entry door, sitting on the steps and chatting about old times, remembering members both gone and still kicking, spying and fish-eyeing one another for mood and unspoken innuendos.

"Come on in, son, come on in." I followed him into the dungeon, the place we called the lower floor, as he asked about Mom. "How is she doing?"

"She's good and likes the retirement village," I said, "Doesn't have to cook as much since Dad's gone."

Jesse packed a new round of tobacco into his curled-stem pipe. He still had that old round pocket watch and chain attached to his vest. "I remember you giving me all those silver dollars, Jesse, those bright silver dollars every Sunday," I said.

"When you was just a sprout, boy," said Jesse. For a while, we sat in silence on folding chairs outside the door of the janitor's closet. As he puffed in reflection, I peered into the fellowship hall, where church members gathered after the morning's service. Jesse's long and yellowed fingernails—yellowed from years of packing tobacco—had assumed more of a brownish tint.

I mentioned the obvious. "And you still got that pipe, Jesse." He laughed and smiled while taking a quick glance at his watch and extended its chain, allowing it to swing and sway, like a bricklayer's plumb line: *searching for truth.*

JAMES GHOLSON, JR.

Jesse surveyed me for a minute. "How you doing up on the Hill, up at Harrison, Caleb? You doing okay?"

"Good, Jesse—not exceptional—but good. I can do the work, but I ain't setting it on fire or nuttin', jes' good."

"You musta worked last night, but you still here a mite early. Don't lie now—you can tell ol' Jesse the truth. You doin' good, but you ain't smokin' it, right?"

"Exactly."

"Worried 'bout some *thang*, like a woman?"

"Nope, that ain't it."

"OK, then, might it be money?"

"A little bit. I hate to stress out Mom, and I don' wanna take out loans. The main thing is—well, *knowing, defining* what is my dream—fame? fortune? Dr. King had a dream; Malcolm had a dream; I don' feel like—that my dream is all the way in place for me. I'm not sure I feel inspired, *manic*—like there is a sprint that I have to race for, something I got to *win* outta this."

"Not sure I can help you wid' that, Caleb. I don't know your field well enough, and wins can be defined in quantities and qualities. One edge you might be needin' to sharpen is a psychological one; one that polishes your ability to think in three dimensions: 3-D! But I *can* help you with de money part. C'mon, li'l brother, follow me."

"Okay. I plan to see my dean later. He wants to have a career talk with me. I'll keep you posted on how it turns out and bring you my next grade report, bring it right here if you promise to ring those church bells for me." Jesse looked over his shoulder at me and smiled.

Jesse was moving now, leaving a long trail of bluish smoke behind him. "You still want to become an architect?"

"Of course," I said matching him stride for stride down the first flight of stairs. He was in his late seventies, but became athletic when necessary.

"You think old Jesse forgets, but old Jesse remembers what he wants to—forgets what he needs to—that's why he's still around. Gonna show you my special project, my archaeological digs."

"Well, I love the design portions of my curriculum, could do better in the drafting and engineering categories," I said.

Jessie stopped and took out a small tamper. "You've become quite a male specimen, Caleb; you look good, you're smart, you got it goin' on. There are so many wonderful stories in history and architecture, Caleb. Historical stories that you youngsters don' know nuttin' about, especially regarding the transitions inside of black history—slave codes, black codes, coffles, contraband—and your ancestors kept them from you because the memories were incredibly painful; wanted you to have a fresh start—no mental hobbles. This is my—our—secret place. Not a word to anyone!" He was galloping down the stairs now, almost disappearing into darkness and pipe smoke, as fast as wobbly knees could run. We descended yet another flight and a half of stairs. From a tall, metallic cabinet, he drew out a long electrician's flashlight catching his breath in slow heaves.

He aimed the broad beam of light at the door, selected a key from a sheath of keys he wore around his waist, and slipped it into a lock affixed to a chain. Once released, his second key—after considerable jiggling—slipped into the tall, metal door. We stepped into a room, both dark and damp, that appeared—at first glance—to be an archaeological dig, replete with wooden stakes, trowels, connectors made of string, labels to mark and delineate grids, and several sifting screens. The cool room smelled of rich, black dirt, and sported low plumbing pipes under which we ducked. It was organized with a surgeon's precision and labeled with the microscopic efficiency of a government bureaucrat.

On the slanted greenhouse window hung several large spiderwebs. I took a seat on a large, veined mound of dirt. Under the window were shelves from which Jesse took one fat burlap bag and opened a large wooden box—a coffin?—from which he gathered fistfuls of china, jewelry, teapots, candelabras, and all manner of utensils, much of it silver.

"Get that door, Caleb ... moving this stuff is kinda noisy," said Jesse. He started digging around his "garden" for two or three minutes. Into the sack went silver cups, chalices, and two golden candelabras, silver trays. "Enough," he said, putting the burlap sack into a rusted, metal suitcase. At the far edge of the suitcase stood a globe-shaped, yellowish, egg-white figure—*an elephant tusk?* It lacked detail in the musty darkness of Jesse's "dig." I sneezed before I could get a good look. When I focused to look again, the suitcase was closed.

"You got a cell phone?" he said. I nodded. "Call a cab so you can get this stuff to your place, and guard this suitcase with your life. This is your trust. When you get home, take pictures of it, and get yourself a safe deposit box pronto. There's a pistol in with that shit too; I checked, it's not loaded. Don't ask me no *questions* now, just get moving. You'll have plenty questions later—stuff be my gift to you—spend it wisely."

The suitcase was heavy, but I got it up all those stairs. Jesse was wasted when we got to the top flight, breathing real heavy and hacking a good bit. "You okay?" I said.

"Hell, boy, I'm fit as a fiddle. Lookee here and remember: you never get truth and faith at the same time, though somehow, they seem to *energize* each other. But when one's around, the other ain't! Listen, your cab's out there! Take care, Caleb, and watch out for your mom; your daddy was crazy about that woman."

Questions! My mind was crazy with questions . . . questions forward, questions backward, upside down. My hands trembled as if they were trapped in a cold, deep freeze, even though the rest of me was in a sweat. I lifted the case into the cab gently. The clasps were rickety and crusted. I waved to Jesse out the back window feeling confused but expectant, thankful and anxious. As the cab headed up toward Florida Avenue, questions popped in my mind like popcorn kernels exploding in a microwave. *Where did all that stuff come from? Why did he keep it buried in the lower recesses of a church? How long had the stuff been there? Why was his garden designed to look like an archaeological dig?*

IV

My eyes became adjusted to daylight brightness as we made our way to campus. "Harrison University," I said to the cabbie, speaking to the back of her Redskins cap, her eyes catching me in the rearview mirror. I had an hour left before my appointment with Dean Davenport. Thinking backward, I chastised myself for taking so few pictures of Jesse's "dig." My emotions stretched past the beat of my heart in two directions; faster, because the gifts that Jesse had bestowed on me were signs that he had confidence in my abilities; slower, because I needed to secure the stuff and find out any negative circumstances surrounding Jesse's gifts. The cab ride was too bumpy to re-create the scene in sketches, but I had time to drop off the suitcase at my apartment before my appointment with Dean Davenport. It would be really silly to strut across campus with this fat, floppish suitcase. Better to stow it before going to see the dean.

JAMES GHOLSON, JR.

I examined the two or three shots I had taken of Jesse's amateur "dig." There were the neatly constructed squares—rowed, columned, and marked with stakes and string. They included pockmarks of holes and dirt dug by Jesse—revealing pieces of metallic artifacts, shelves of boxes filled to the gills and carefully housing all sorts of small gardening tools: picks, small shovels, cans, jars, and rope. For some reason, I wondered if Jesse secretly wanted to become an archaeologist. Had he taken classes in archeology? All the basic tools were there: shovels, sifting screens, brushes, notebooks, picks, and wooden stakes (for *vampires?*). I knew enough about the field to know that, like everything else, technology had made a ton of changes to the way "archies" functioned. *But, hey, could it be a signal that his spirit yet maintained the psyche of past times, segregated, a-part-ness and relegated to the provincial? (There was not a computer in sight.)*

"Do you have a street address?" said my cabbie. I gave my apartment address with a look both bewildered and surprised. We'd made better time than I thought. "You handle this traffic like a magician," I said.

"Thanks," she responded.

"I'll pay you double if you wait for me to lug this thing up to my apartment. I have to go to the Architecture Building on campus."

"Okay," said my cabbie, "no problem."

I made it to Dean Davenport's office five minutes before my appointment time of three o'clock. It took me a minute or so outside his office before I could remember his secretary's name: Arabelle.

"Ms. Arabelle," I said, "I have an appointment to see the dean."

She smiled, "Oh yes, he is expecting you," and she directed me to a seat on the opposite wall, while alerting him to my presence on her phone.

Think in three dimensions crept through my thoughts as I waited. Were these words another gift, a gift learned through living that Jesse had given me? So many gifts, and I felt as though the material ones given were those of fruit stolen.

"Well, Caleb Fentress," bellowed Dean Davenport as he broached the doorway of his inner office. "It's a pleasure to see you; come right in and have a seat." He had appeared out of the shadows of its dark interior. "Sit over there by the window so I can see you, young man, so I can see you ... Sight ain't what it used to be."

"Hi, Dean," I said. There was meekness in my voice. "Good to see you also."

"Do you drink coffee, son?"

"Yes sir, though I missed mine this morning."

"Well, you got here just in time. I always have a sip around this time. Have a cup with me."

"Yes sir, I'd be proud to join you," I said.

"Arabelle," he said on the phone, "—hate to bother you. Would you—exactly, and—you are such a kind soul." I could hear her speak through the phone, filling in his silences. "If you ever get to choose a secretary, use Arabelle as your model—she is absolutely perfect. Now, Caleb, I've been watching you for some time . . . must say that you are not the easiest person to understand. You have done good work here in school, a good solid citizen and an exceptional talent. Your professors all say you have exceptional ability, but perhaps restrained—*constrained*—in some unique way. Your grades are *good*, actually better than I might have guessed, but perhaps, overall, your effort seems uninspired."

"Thank you, sir. I appreciate your comments. Coming from you—"

"I know you are trying, and trying is indeed a good thing. My own experience says to me that trying sometimes needs inspiration to shatter barriers, real or imagined, self-imposed or imposed from societal—let us say, *mores*—to reach the level of artistic accomplishment. Down South, where I'm from, young black guys drop girlfriends off at the campus gate, use their girl's car all day, and pick them up after class, never stepping foot on the campus. Ten years later, the same young lady will sue for domestic violence! Grit and grind are fine, but I'm talking about intellectual effort that produces real *wonder-in-the-miraculous,* Caleb. You have the kind of ability that can accomplish a great vision. Somewhere between past and future, once you get dialed in to your vision, calibrate and bring that vision to fruition. I feel in my bones that you are capable of great architecture."

As I listened, the battery of my soul fired cannons at my contrived reasons—excuses, really, I had come up with for shielding my eyes from the extraordinary, from miraculous vision. My pride was wounded by this truth, even as monetary issues had been removed—or would be—by Jesse's surprising support. Jesse's pocket watch—*golden, hypnotic, swinging back and forth*—still held me in its orbit of gravity. The words virtually exploded around me, my pulse rate galloped like snare drums galloping my emotions past the boiling point. *Shithead, I don't aspire to greatness; I just need a paycheck. Greatness draws jealously, hatred, controversy. Fuck that!* I wanted to shoot this messenger.

"I want—"

"Gentlemen, excuse me," said Arabelle, "your coffee is ready, and I don't want it served cold. I already added cream and sugar, one each. Anything else?" We both shook our heads in the negative.

"Dean, I understand what you are saying, and you are correct. There is something gnawing at my resolve, a doughnut hole in my belief that I can achieve the extraordinary. I am working on it. My grades are up even from last year. I know I rarely race full-out, open throttle, to compete. I have revised my study techniques with flash cards and efficient reading. I am more immersed in my subjects, and think I can grind this out."

Davenport's bow tie flexed around his neck, and I fish-eyed him sliding back in his chair. On opposite walls of his office were pictures of Dr. Martin and Malcolm X in black and white. "Your professors see promise in you, Caleb," he said lifting his feet to his desktop, a broad grin crawling across his face.

"Lemme cut to the chase, Caleb. I understand the grind *and* the trot. You know old General George Thomas—the man honored by that statue up at Thomas Circle? Some nicknamed him 'Slow Trot.' He refused to be rushed into battle; refused to let control of his battle plan be wrestled from his strategic vision, the keyword being *vision*. Because he was a Northerner, Lincoln trusted Grant more than Thomas. At the Second Battle of Nashville, Grant almost replaced Thomas with General John Logan. Thomas was beloved by his men throughout his command. His men felt great confidence in his thoroughness of preparation, and confidence in his strategic vision. Now at this stage of your development, I have an opportunity I want to present to you. It will provoke both your vision of self and your vision of architecture. We are looking for a student to participate as an architectural extern with the Greek government. It lasts for under two months. This student gets all expenses paid for those weeks—free housing and food, and free tickets to concerts in the Acropolis. Your job will be to help around the museum offices—promotion, docent presentations, odd jobs—anything that comes up. Assist and support. It's called the Acropolis Project. Are you interested?"

The Acropolis! I'd seen pictures of the new Acropolis Museum. My jaw bounced off my knees and slammed against my upper molars. "Yes sir, very interested, sir." I felt like a young cadet sketching a salute. My spirit sang "Hallelujah," and my mouth stole a march under stunned eyes saying, "I'll sign up right now!"

"Now if this goes through and you end up there, take advantage of some group, even individual classes—oils, tempura, water colors—whatever it takes to clearly document your vision. I have a talisman for you, some sketches and blueprints, as small gifts of *creative* intrigue for personal stimulation. Arabelle will fill out the paperwork, so check back with us in a week or so; just sign at the bottom as you leave." He handed me a large brown envelope. "Congratulations, Caleb. Here's a cigar if you care to celebrate. If you don't smoke, hang it on the wall! Now, be sure to give Arabelle your cell number, e-mail, and street address." I shook Dean's hand and smiled at Arabelle.

"Congratulations, Caleb," she said. "Here's a pen and the back page for your signature. I'll send you a reminder via text. Hang that stinky cigar on the wall or you'll get sick!"

V

"Hey, Sam," I chirped, "whassup?"
"I waited for you, Caleb . . . Thought you were going to call me, thought maybe something had happened to you!"

Samantha, the first great love of my life, was in my apartment when I returned from Davenport's office. She was the blessed owner of a pair of the most beautiful, golden-tan legs that the city campus of Harrison University had ever seen. We had become lovers during her second, my third year on campus. Occasionally, she would stay over—to study, of course, and make brownies—until raging hormones were too furious to resist . . . *Has she seen the skull?* It remained as before, draped beneath the towel and bordered by the book fortress around it. *Whew!*

"Nope, all good," I said with nonchalance. "You have a bit of a sparkle in your eye, Sam," and we played kiss and tug, with her mussing my hair childishly.

Sam could wax a bit frantic when frightened. I knew that the skull, if discovered, could tip her over the edge.

"My day has been a tumble of surprises; it's good to see you . . . Feel better already." Sam's calm demeanor reassured me, and I added, "Didn't see anything on my phone from you." Several long breaths took me into calm relief from my fear that she might stumble into those objects.

"Well, give me the rundown, Caleb. What have you been up to? Tell me about this tumble of surprises," she said.

For some reason, I started thinking of how much help she could have been in aiding me to clean all that crap up . . . silver buried in dirt, candelabras buried in dirt, and burlap bags covered in dirt. *Brother, are you stupid!* I thought to myself. But if you ever *saw* Sam operate on a fly or mosquito, you would know that she could be furious in pursuit of the pest, singularly determined that it would not survive.

"I'll tell you all about it, hon. Come over here, sit by me, and rest your sweet li'l head on my shoulder," I said. "I went to see my dad's friend Jesse at New Canaan Baptist, the church my family attended over in Northeast. I was feeling a little down and needed to chat a bit about stuff, so we talked for a good while, just about old times. I started to roll by the frat house, play some whist with some of the regulars—you know, Benny and Kashmir always are around drinking a few beers or playin' the dozens like they're stranded somewhere between outer space and the Mississippi—but I had that meet with the dean—"

"You had a meet with the dean?" she said with excitement. "Was he pissed with you or something?—I know a couple of folks who just hate that old sucker! And one of my sorority friends thinks that he is a perfect ass; probably beats his wife. He just looks so old-school and proper: *mean.*" She threw her arms around me, jibing me with a barrage of kisses and said, "Poor baby, so what happened? Did he give you the chew for one of your drawings or a paper?"

"Oh no, it was a good meet. He gave me a pep talk about my ability and—*dare I say anything about the extern proposal?*—encouraged me to stay the course. I think he has my best interests at heart. He even offered me a cigar! Here, you want it?" Her head shake was notably negative, and I shot her a smile. "He's really a nice man, and we ended up talking career talk. Stuff about what I plan to do after I graduate. He went to Harrison as an undergraduate and spoke about hearing Martin King and Malcolm X and witnessing them back in the day. You could feel his commitment to the allocation of historical models, the tension between black nationalistic and integrationists in Afro-American cultural philosophy. He mentioned some guy named Abele. *The last thing I want to deal with is her being upset about me being out of town during the summer; out of the country, really.* Got to do some research on him; suspect he was an architect. Anyway, he gave me some stuff to look over."

"You mean he thinks you disrespect black architects—architecture by blacks?" said Sam.

"Well, it's more a sin of omission than anything else. It's more like he wants me to understand how others forged a path to success. My impression is that he wants me to choose models and mentors that light my way. And there are many avenues to professional growth, so perhaps it's nothing more than being aware of architecture on an international scale and the challenges faced by black architects in this country. He wants to be sure I am aware of what has been accomplished by black architects of the past. I mean, you can't really disrespect what you don't know about; that would be kinda stupid on my part," I said. Perplexed for a moment, Sam looked at me as if I had addressed *her* with the "N" word.

"Well, sounds almost like philosophy instead of architecture," said Sam. "Anyway, Jackie came by the sorority house in the late afternoon, and we talked about the serenade and what we would wear, and all.

SKULLY

I have some pink slacks that would be perfect!" There was an earnestness in her voice that drew my eyeballs away from the shadows in which that skull lay, an earnestness which snapped my ears to attention. Our sweetheart, who was in her sorority, would be serenaded next week by me and my frat bothers. For the present, my ramblings kept her state calm, if mildly confused.

"Oh yeah. I meant to kibbutz with the good brothers about that too." Actually, my degree curriculum at school had become much more intense, and I couldn't drop by as much. A few of the brothers who grooved on tokes, bid-whist, and the kibbutz, had lately found themselves trapped in a rut: *Boston!* "And, I've got to memorize the sweetheart's song. Say, are you hungry? Why don't we order a pizza—vegetarian?" I said.

Sam found some coupons in her purse. She called the corner pizza joint, ordered, and paid for a large vegetarian. "Okay, thanks," she said to the store operator. "Pizza's on the way," she added, looking at me. "So, Dapper Davenport heard speeches at Rankin Hall by those guys back in the sixties . . . back in the day of Stokely and Rap Brown. I wonder what they would think now, seeing brothers in the street shootin' each other at a record pace."

"Now that hell-fired question is what lots of folks

ask. The answer probably falls into the category of economics, peppered with psychology, history, and buttered with survival. That, followed by unending diatribes about personal commitment and social circumstances," I said. I felt happy—glad I had barricaded the skull on the bookcase, glad that it was covered too. I stooped to kiss Sam on her cheek, poured beer, and we devoured the pizza as soon as it arrived.

We lay on the bed in my bedroom, still talking as Sam slipped out of her jeans; the warmth of our hormones practically lit up the room. Occasionally, we would look out across D.C., at the skyline of the nation's capital, study the chalky, steadfast luminescence of the rotunda's exterior. "You know, that building is the brains of the nation; it's where imagination and problems meet to find solutions," I said. "Talking to Jesse was great; he was jus' kinda hangin' out smokin' his pipe and mentioning how much he respects the young man I have become, the effort that I've put into my studies, and my embrace of the unknown. I shoulda got his telephone number ... Forgot to do that."

We kissed for a long time now, joyful in the feel of each other, spurred by the agitation of "dem hormones," and expectant in the pleasures and ceremonies of rituals yet to be played in surprising explorations and rhythms; rituals that inaugurated spectacular delicacies, revealed pathways of delicious delight, release, and spellbound satisfaction. I held Sam with firm gentleness as she quaked once, then twice. Her moments were spectacular to witness in touch and focused: body quakes.

Later, we quaked together. When I rose to brush my pizza-covered teeth, I opened windows throughout my apartment. A soft rain had started. Sam slept soundly, and above the pitter-patter of raindrops, I heard soft arpeggios—like a flute whispering somewhere—and moved to investigate. The detective in me tiptoed, first to the bathroom, to the vicinity of the front door, then to the book-fortress where I'd stashed the skull—strangely minus the towel formerly draped over it. I put my hand—palm down—over the hole in its crown. *The sounds stopped!* The arpeggios, spawned from breezes outside the window, sounded as if blown across the aperture of the hole in the skull's crown. *Jeez!* I purloined one of Sam's cigarettes, thinking of the ideas, sounds—words I had *not* shared with her: nothing incisive about Malcolm or Martin, nothing about Jesse's quasi-archaeological dig, nothing about the rage in the black faces of Basquiat, nothing about the increasing number of Americans—black and white—with licenses to carry—*nothing* about the skull. As I remounted my bed, Sam wound her arms around my waist and in no time flat, we erupted once more.

VI

"*See you later*" read the note Sam left; she was gone by the time I awakened. I studied the ceiling, fingers woven behind my noggin, thoughts floating inside my head on clouds. Samantha had left before we could chat or sketch out the day. *Communication my doughnut hole? A refusal to examine joy by daylight? Do the joys of the night echo hollow and brainless by daylight?* I'd discussed the possibility of study in Greece with no one—not Mom, not a frat brother, not Samantha. I was thrilled about the possibility, gussied with joy. *Is this strange? Fearful of failure, bro; simple answer, crow when the deal is real and not befo'!*

The good brothers of my frat were in a bit of a quandary. We all knew the facts, but it was not something we openly discussed. Our Polemarch had flipped, come out of the closet, and arched eyebrows met brothers as they trekked across campus to class.

We would serenade our sweetheart next week; her sorority wanted to serenade our Polemarch in reciprocity. *What to do?*

I made some coffee just as my personal what-to-dos hit me. *Drag that suitcase into the bathroom, open it, run soapy hot water in the tub, and rinse everything off.* I had coffee stinking up the apartment real good when I spied my lonely looking skull. I took a selfie with it and looked around for a box to protect it. Once found, I lined it with old newspapers and packing peanuts as additional barriers. Several old *Sunday Posts* and old shirts packed leftover space. With selfies taken, the skull boxed, coffee made and drained, I dipped (in soapy water) and dried every item in the suitcase (with the exception of the pistol, those loose manuscript pages, a hymnal, and one loose music page reading "To Canaan"). I reexamined the items: forks, knives, spoons, candelabras, trays, tea and coffee pots, coins, rings, chalices. There was an array of dazzling silver stuff. I oiled the latches of Jesse's suitcase and lined the suitcase with towels; each item was placed inside. Jesse's gift to me could probably finance whatever classes I might need to finish my degree work, maybe more. After draining a second cup of coffee, I called a cab.

At the bank, I opened an account for a large deposit box, placing all items inside it. I felt better and took a deep breath. That done, I walked the cardboard box containing the skull toward the Anatomy Department.

Who are you? Where do you come from? Are you a murder victim? Are you male or female? Did Jesse commit a crime of some sort? Questions about the skull teased every step I took. When I reached the door to the main office, I could hardly remember the route I had taken to get there. I spoke to the secretary. "Hi, my name is Caleb Fentress. I'm a student here at Harrison and—uh—uh—found this box—*in an old car I bought? in my apartment's laundry room?*—beside the Dumpster behind my apartment. I wanted—"

A middle-aged woman got up from her desk and walked over toward me. "You found what? What's in the box?" she said, "and you are?"

Another woman, younger, walked through the door in a lab coat and stood at the side of the waist-high visitor's panel.

"Fentress, Caleb Fentress. Uh, I found this beside the Dumpster and wanted somebody to get it looked at."

The second woman starting helping me unbox the skull, lifting it out with steady, long fingers. "Well, well," she said studying the bony structure, "this little guy or gal had some bad thing happen. It looks like it's been soaked in water a good bit, been about for some time in its current state. We might have to keep it for a while to study this 'skull-in-a -box' and run several tests ... DNA and such ... and perhaps make an identification."

The secretary had stepped backward, away from the box as the younger one lifted it upward. A pale look of horror consumed her from the neck up. I noticed a faint scent of formaldehyde.

The woman in the lab coat spoke next. "You want to know if you will be charged with murder?" The smirk on her face subsided, and she added, "No, at least not yet. Normally, we do not accept items like this; certainly we will have to call the coroner or police."

"Did you say you are a student?" said the secretary.

"Yes, ma'am; Caleb Fentress." My knees trembled at the Dumpster lie I'd told. I didn't want to mention anything about Jesse.

"But since you are a student," said the younger woman in the lab coat, "we'll work on this for you. You'll probably need to tell the authorities more about how you came across this, about your—hmm ... acquisition." She wrote on the top of a form and gave me several forms to fill out and sign.

"Lara," said the secretary, fingers trembling as she wrote, "Mr. Harrison here lives on Fentress."

"That's not quite right," I said, adding, "I'm a student here at Harrison; my *name* is Fentress—Caleb

Fentress." I filled out the paperwork she'd handed me; date, contact info, signature, and checked for all tests to be run. "Who are you?" I said, speaking in the direction of the lab coat.

"Lara Fields. Good to meet you." We shook hands. "These tests will take awhile, so you'll have to leave this item with us. Since you're here, I have several boxes I'm taking over to the Admin Building. Can you give me a hand with some of these? It will only take a few minutes." Light freckles peppered her face, and she exhibited the clear, focused actions of a young woman serious about her work. Out of her pocket came an inch-wide artist's brush. With it, she applied light strokes to the skull.

"If I was going to apply a name, I'd call it Skully. That way, we can call her Skullie if it's a girl." She slipped Skully, or Skullie, back inside the box. "Let me get a receipt for you so you feel comfortable. We'll take good care of your skull. We'll make some notes—as I said, we will have to notify district authorities—and give you all the information we collect. We will try to come up with a careful identification, perhaps even more information about it than you ever wanted to know."

"Okay, happy to help," I said following her to a stack of boxes. Lara came back quickly and handed me a receipt.

SKULLY

Ms. Fields pointed to the boxes she wanted me to carry, and I lifted them. Determined not to allow my nervousness to show, I lifted two boxes and she one, and we were off to deliver her boxes at the Administration Building. Questions zoomed around inside my head, swarming like flies; my knees felt trembly. *Is this someone Jessie knew? Where is Jesse from? Good God, I hope Jesse didn't kill somebody—heck, I didn't bargain for all this. Maybe Mom knows how to contact Jesse. I might have made a mistake by accepting the skull, might have a mistake accepting all of it!* Now my stomach started churning. For a moment, I saw Jesse's pocket watch undulate. A bloom of air rushed in from outside as she held open the doors, and I took in several breaths of fresh air. *Ah, that's better. Maybe it was the formaldehyde!*

"You know you cannot get in trouble for bringing in body parts; they get found a lot. Usually, the authorities prefer that you leave them in place, but, golly, when you see something like this, you want to make it safe, put it in a safe place. I mean, everybody finds stuff that surprises and shocks; otherwise, there would be no detective stories." Lara said, "What's your major, Mr. Fentress ... May I call you Caleb?"

"Oh yes, for sure. I was a *borderline* architectural student, now somewhat reformed and trending committed," I said, talking around the boxes.

JAMES GHOLSON, JR.

"So architecture is your first love?" she said.

"Well, if you put it that way, maybe. I'm still figuring that out," I replied.

"Did you really find that skull or perhaps come across it another way?"

"Why would you think that? I tried to be honest with you guys. Frankly, skulls scare me half to death. I had it in my apartment last night, and the damn thing was whistling, almost singing!"

We were halfway to the Admin Building now, and I'd seen some frat brothers, some kids off the block, several former classmates, and nodded or spoke to them.

"You always speak to strangers?" she said.

"Sonar survival," I said. "My way of knowing the nature of my environment, what is threatening, what's not. I know some of those folks. One of those guys is our Polemarch. He just came out, so I wanted to be sure to acknowledge him. He might be getting teased a bit, mostly behind his back. Usually, I can tell from tone, articulation, affability, what is threatening and what's not. Gives me a sorta quick 'character-photo' of the people I'm around. It's kinda a basketball thing, where you size up folks quickly for the enterprise at hand. You don't want a pickup game with some dude so screwed up that he wants to shoot you for winning. Like a random encounter—"

"With a skull?" said Lara.

"I guess you could say that, but I sure don't want to *be* one. Anyway, skulls don't shoot! And they don't follow you home if you win. I've played random contests—pickup basketball—all over D.C. You also get to learn how good or lousy your skills are, see various fresh moves, and such. Mostly, though, respect begets respect. You give it, your get it, and you go home with lessons learned; new ways to improve your game. What's your major?" I said.

"I'm in forensic science. I enjoy using my wits and technology to figure things out."

"You from around here?"

"Nope . . . Came to Harrison from Philadelphia. I have enjoyed my Harrison experience."

"Did you come for the program or a particular professor?"

"Maybe a bit of both. My high school English teacher had been a detective and drove a bunch of us down from Philly. She had side interests in archeology and some of us worked with her in the summers on Civil War sites. She adored my major prof."

"Really?"

"Yep. Okay, we're here, if you get the door, I'm all set. Give us at least two weeks to get some test results back. We have your information and will be in touch with you. Thanks, Caleb!"

"Nice chatting, Ms. Fields; be good to yourself."
"Call me Lara."

So Skullie, or Skully, had a name—no brain—but a name. Jessie's gifts seemed unique now, a double-barreled mixed blessing. The metal could be translated into cash, and perhaps a fair amount of it. The thought that Jessie might be a killer, a lethal personality, had never crossed my mind! Strange things happen reasonably often, but finding skulls without spines, or brains with hearts, deserves more than honorable mention. Then again, even in my young life, I had witnessed brains without hearts—hearts without brains too. Ditto for brainless spines and spineless brains. *Have I been dumped on by Jesse as a cover-up for a crime?* The thought stood in a dark corner and pouted as if to say, "Over here, big boy—over here!" A bold shadow! I thought of our Polemarch again. *Simple answer, that's his issue to crow about—or not crow about—not mine!*

VII

There are reasons, beyond respect, that I made it a practice to acknowledge the presence of others as I moved across campus. Most of the individuals I saw were members of the Harrison community. I knew them. I use language as sonar also because it tells me info about temperament, background, psychology, self-respect, and respect for others. Language sonar gives me snippets of personality; valuable on the streets of D.C. or any metropolitan area. It is a great gift of playing pickup basketball. If you are in for, let's say, a butt whuppin', it is a good idea to know that it is on the way and who is bringing it. It's merely a matter of a verbal "Yo, bro," or "Whassup?" here and there. Under normal circumstances, the least articulate, least socially and financially confident, and most frustrated dude on the corner is the one who deserves the most attention, in terms of violent physicality. That's the why of common vernacular used by me, first, down Georgia, then toward New Hampshire Avenue to the frat house, Tuesday after class. It was three o'clock in the afternoon.

You can't get to the frat house in a straight line; only winged creatures—like crows—can do that. I can't say if their intergenerational memories assist them on the level of sonar language, but I was surprised to learn their memories do assist them in remembering lousy interactions with humans *intergenerationally!* I used my own minimal skills. On my way west, I was passed by a small, yellow Volkswagen which stopped and honked.

"Hey, brown sugar! Where are you going? Need a lift?"

I went over to the car and hugged Candy, whom I knew from some of my classes. Candy could work difficult math and algebra problems in her head without lifting a pencil. Western sunlight enhanced the shape of her round face and beamed off the car, but tree shadows scumbled and obscured the backseat riders.

I caught a whiff of weed coming from the rear and noticed some of her sisters and Trevor Gordon, one of my frat brothers. Candy had a cherry blossom in her hair, and the girls giggled as we spoke. Trevor smoked a blunt.

"We're headed to the house for the serenade; you can ride on the bumper, Caleb," she said jesting.

"Might be a kinda rough ride," I said, "but I'll see you guys there. Are you folks going to sing?" I said. "Samantha hipped me to the serenade."

"We'll be gone by the time you get there walking," she said. "Yeah, but I've got to exercise these legs so I can sing to you tonight—you and Samantha."

Candy smiled and popped the clutch.

On the street, you could feel the anticipation of spring in the air, like the collective blooming of all living agencies; the trees, the azaleas, the budding cherry blossoms. Tree leaves had already exposed themselves in minute shapes.

My pledge line had called themselves the "Iron Brigade," troopers for freedom. As a fraternity, we loved the camaraderie of joining other bright students from all over the country, pursuing careers newly accessible to us—at least theoretically. We intended to show our capabilities as buppies . . . brown, upwardly mobile, meritorious. We would spit in the eye of slavery and Jim Crow segregation. Questions about Skully yet perplexed me, and Jesse's comment, "'Cuz we always be the onliest ones that gots to think in '3-D,' past, future and present all at once."

"Caleb, my brother, how you be, guy?" said Marcus,

one of the regulars at Harrison from Pittsburgh. A theater and art major, our paths crossed often on campus. "Everybody's excited, and, man, the girls are all cranked up. You seen Trevor lately?"

"Yeah, just saw him riding with Candy sporting that snobbish sneer on his face," I said.

"Man, he caned some of our pledges the other day something awful; it was like he was another person!" said Marcus.

"Guess he's just being his 'BS' self," I said, reflecting on Trevor's bemused looks toward Candy. "It's all good, Marcus, all good," I said.

I hobnobbed with brothers I hadn't seen in a while, got a cup of lemonade laced with Beefeater's vodka, and practiced harmonizing with a few of the better singers. The Brookland pledges sang with us, adding voices and vibrancy to our efforts. We sounded really good. After the quick practice, I whispered to Marcus, "Trying to get my ducks in a row, man. Sorry I haven't been around more. The books have got me all cornered up, dude."

Castro ran around the card table in absolute ecstasy, yelling, "Boston, y'all," as Terry and his partner rose from their card stint. Castro had the ace of spades stuck to his forehead, just a little lower than that hole in Skully's crown. He said, "Don't nobody get real comfortable now. Keep your wings on, so's you can rise easy and quick: *painless!* Lady Luck is mine today!"

Most of our guys were present, but I didn't see Candy and her crew. Just then, Trevor, a cock-eyed grin on his face, said, "Candy says the girls have a little surprise for us—said they would be marching to the house from down the street. The big sisters want us to make a big circle, and their pledges are going to sing right after we serenade our sweetheart."

Outside, the brothers gathered around in a huge circle—some on the steps beside me, others beyond the fence.

A large crowd of onlookers, folks just getting off work and fellow collegians and neighbors interested in seeing what the fuss was all about, on both sides of the street, listened, as our Polemarch introduced Felicity Jones, our lovely sweetheart. She was dressed to the nines. Our pledges, singing a tune called "Rebels of Innovation," hipped and hopped down "S" Street, lead dog in the front and accompanied by a drum-line from the university band. We sang the sweetheart song—which was harmonized beautifully—in the warmth of bass, baritone, and lyrical tenor voices, from the depths of our souls. The crowd gave us thunderous applause. The place seemed hallowed, descended upon by a huge human tidal wave. I still couldn't find Samantha in the crowd, thinking, *Wow, Samantha is missing all this.*

Before the sorority pledges were to do their thing, our fraternity pledges broke ranks from our circle and leaped into a hip-hop version of the sweetheart's song. The crowd, jabbering from shock into awe, was riveted to the show. Not only were the hip-hoppers coordinated in movement, they executed their steps with pinpoint precision. When their serenading was done, we all waited to see the show put on by the pledges of Sam's sorority.

"Oh, look!" a single sentry shouted. A commotion brewed just down the street, and the eyes of the crowd started to shift to an area just west of the frat house. We heard some drumming—African drummers to be exact—and from around the corner came a long, lime-green Chinese dragon, bobbing and bopping to the rhythm of the drums. Children playing in yards up and down the street froze in their steps and shimmied down the street to better see the ceremony. Believe it or not, the dragon turned the corner and made its way—with huge oversized nostrils nodding and exhaling fire past its red tongue—to just beyond where we stood. I stepped to the top of the stairs to see better. Out of that yellow Volkswagen seen earlier popped Sam in a *fireman's* uniform. The crowd clamored, gleefully taking pictures of collegians at play.

Even buses and cabs had stopped to see what was going on. From the corner of my eye, I saw Candy and Trevor rush forth holding a long, blueish fire hose.

With the suddenness of a panther, Samantha—her face flushed, wrenched into a hideous glare, sleeves rolled up to her shoulders and lipstick askew—appeared from behind Candy's Volkswagen. *Has she been there the whole time?* She bounded past rows of working stiffs holding lunch pails, raced to the head of the hose, lifted its shaft from Candy's hands, and flipped the nozzle, releasing an onslaught of water. Sam drew back and threw my apartment key towards *me*. Her throw pitched me into mental confusion. It was my key; I had attached a huge metal "C" to it. Buoyed by a ferocious torrent of spray from the water hose, the key rode toward me, tumbling, tossing, and finally *cresting* just in front of my eyes. Sloshed, I'd managed to track the key's movement, half sidestepped a torrent of water, snatched it fractured between wind and water, lost balance, tumbled down the incline of steps, and into the small yard. Talk about embarrassed! I should have let the key fall, thereby averting the slap of my head on concrete, a wallop and glide! To make matters worse, the foul invective that gushed from Sam's mouth shocked astonished nearby students and office workers disembarking from buses and blue-collar workers

JAMES GHOLSON, JR.

returning from stints at the Navy Yard. Disgusted and red-faced, they promptly turned heel to continue their journey home.

Even as I made my way home, it was hard to imagine any event I'd ever attended, where the tone of it had been so dramatically altered, from a block of admiring participants, collegians, and onlookers, seduced by singing and adoration, to a ruble of vengeance, hatefulness, pity, and spite. Stupefied onlookers ran to avoid being trampled by rabble-rousers and potential hooligans.

When I reached my apartment, I read the loose page of that hymnal which yet lay at the bottom of Jesse's suitcase. What the heck was wrong with Sam?

What troop is this that follows,
All armed with picks and spades?
These are the swarthy bondsmen—
The iron-skin brigades!
They'll pile up Freedom's breastwork,
They'll scoop out rebels' graves;
Who then will be their owner
And march them off for slaves?
To Canaan, to Canaan
The Lord has led us forth,
To strike upon the captive's chain
The hammers of the North!

VIII

To my dismay, pictures of my tumble found their way into the local newspapers. Embarrassment on this high a level was new to me. I freely participated in class discussions and critiques, turned my papers in on time, and did all the basic things necessary to academic success. Uninspired, I was a methodical student. My emotions were the seat of a swing, tracing an arc of polarities—inwardly enraged, outwardly stoic—and reminded me of the swing and sway of Jesse's golden pocket watch: first Martin's peace, then Malcolm's rage. Giggles pockmarked the air when I strolled across campus. At least during my daily pilgrimages to and fro, pride glowed from my quiet news: to be in line for a summer externship in Greece: *Hallelujah!* At the same time, I felt the sting of social failure, falling further into my psychic doughnut hole, anchored at the lowest rung of black-Greek social society. I countered social embarrassment with a large dose of separation. When my phone rang, I ignored it; when a knock on my door came, I let it pass; when I was notified of frat meetings, I skipped them. In short, I curtailed almost all socializing. The best part was that I became a better student. How? I focused on doing better work. I attended study groups and finagled a tutor; I asked detailed questions. I read more intensely (with questions and wisecracks in the margins), and I concerned myself with how I would pursue employment after graduation.

Both campus and local newspapers treated the abortive serenade with hilarity. The times of "Tumbleweed" became the topic of TV and radio discussions; pictures of the Chinese dragon—replete with the stories of our sweetheart's reaction to the hubbub. Fashion statements followed: the Tumbleweed Look, the Tumbleweed Shuffle, the Dragonweed Follies, etc. That Chinese dragon's snake up New Hampshire Avenue, hip-hopping to "Be My Baby, Love," through crowds of wide-eyed onlookers and neighbors. My fall captivated the public. Through the eye of my mind, my tumble played like a bad movie, forward and backward, frame by frame, with me trying to freeze the action, erase it, make it disappear. The most frightening frame was of me precipitously poised, stretching to snatch that wet key out of the air. The original purpose of the serenade was subsumed by a tragic pose—comic to many and disastrous to me—that featured me strumming iron banisters as if they were a harp. The caption under the photo consisted of one word: *Tumbleweed!* To make matters worse, I had no inside track or viable facts to understand Sam's angry assertion: "You homosexual, faggot. *Jeez!*" We had been lovers for over a year and a half. To me, she was one of the most physically attractive women I had ever seen—sweet lips, gorgeous hips and legs, and often personally generous. But then, we didn't talk a bunch or debate current events, or even casually attend each other's classes. *Am I pussy-whipped?* If so, I was lovin' it—but nothing like this had ever happened before. I raided my brain for possible scenarios that might impel her public attack against me.

As I upped the ante on my studying, developed drills for left-handed sketching (I am right-handed), started seriously learning Linux and Unix, installed a higher grade of a computer-assisted drawing software, worked to refine my portfolio, and started reading the biographies of several architects, random architects of all ethnicities, not just those black or white. I was in no mood to seek out Jesse to find out where that skull came from or what may have been its lot in life. In short, I burrowed myself in academic purposefulness. *Tumbleweed, my ass,* when someone called, "Hey, Tumbleweed!" The worst shaming came in video versions on the Internet. On campus, I became superanonymous in hoods and shades; that was the look I wore as I sauntered into the Anatomy Department to check on developments with Skully (Skullie).

"You *said* you found this skull outside; tests suggest otherwise. It seems well taken care of. My instincts tell me that your explanation is muddy; it lacks clarity—veracity. Tell me again, in detail—how you came to find it," said Lara.

"Weird stuff *trails* you, not just this Skullie. We saw your picture in the paper and wondered how you were holding up. Oops," she said giggling, "I spoke too loudly. Tumbleweed! Now, that is a striking moniker for sure—if you like that sorta thing."

Some workers in her office had broken into outright laughing. She took my arm and led me away, outside the double doors. As we passed through the doors, I could hear them chatter and laugh. "I know all that must be embarrassing for you. Really, I am sorry. Did you—? Was he or she or it really outside? Were you given this skull—Skullie—by somebody, a frat brother, a friend?" she said quizzically, peeved as I stood, eyes shaded and full of psychic confusion, head hooded before her. I held a lengthy squeamish gaze before responding.

"Look," I said, face shaded, "I promise to tell you the whole story; I can't right now. I just wanted to see what results had come in, where the tests led." I could hear more raucous laughter now. Over my shoulder, I saw a janitor slap his thigh through overalls.

Almost immediately, Lara covered her mouth. "I'm so sorry," she said struggling for composure.

"Don't worry, it's all good. I just came to find out if there are any results on Skully. Have you heard anything?" I said, my inner coolness stepping up.

"We have heard something from Legal Affairs. We did have to report how we, you, found it, and the circumstances, to the police. He—we think he and not she—is quite old, perhaps more than one hundred years old. They seem to have determined and tested for that. But you know how bureaucrats are. They want documentation that no crime has been committed. I'll read their questions to you."

Lara disappeared to retrieve the initial report and reappeared adding, "Where did you find the skull? What were the circumstances? How long has it been in your possession? And do you have any additional knowledge about it?" She surveyed me with a slow fish-eye. "Caleb, did you hurt yourself in that—tumble?" She gave me a big hug as she said that, and we both cracked up. It was the first time I had laughed in a week. I shook my head in the negative, while she stifled a chuckle. "When I saw that picture of the dragon and you tumbling down the steps, I just could hardly believe it. And the caption, 'Tumbleweed!' The entire campus seemed to heave with a unified guffaw. I'm so glad that you're okay. I saw Samantha on campus a few days ago; she seemed a bit morose. Have you—?"

"We haven't spoken; I mean she doesn't return any of my texts or calls. I have no idea what to say to her. I've racked my heart about stuff to ask her, but have no idea how to put it all into words." Lara's eyes appeared to show sincerity in her concern for my welfare. Even the freckles on her face danced about recklessly. "I must be—"

"The campus laughingstock? Not to worry. But what on earth did you do?"

"Honestly, no idea—we've been together for a long while."

"Well, I don't want to pry, and at least you didn't break anything except your pride."

We walked toward the exit of the building. Lara said, "It will all work out; we should have the DNA results back in a week or so. I have all your information and will contact you with any updates." I had already started thinking up my explanation to Dean Davenport of the Tumbleweed newspaper photo. Lara said, "One thing in particular. We have already placed the skull—Skully—in a vacuum bell. That should help preserve it; we did notice the hole in its crown and its jaw is broken—maybe a blow. I'll take some photos and forward them to you. Take care of yourself, Caleb," Lara said disappearing inside the building. I made my way to Dean Davenport's office.

IX

"Amazing, isn't it!" The words popped out of Dean's Davenport's mouth just as Arabelle waved me into his office. "Just talking to an old buddy about that talisman perk I gave you; everything okay?" Dean said, giving me a quick fish-eye.

"Pretty good. I enjoyed researching Abele, though I had never heard of him before."

"Poor soul was internationally trained and couldn't see his own designs as they were physically constructed," said Davenport. "There are times when this country has plunged into the nineteenth, twentieth, and now the twenty-first century ass-first. And this current jackass doesn't know a tit from a turnip! Old Julian couldn't sign his name to his drafts because of a sixteen-year-old dropout. A-*maz*-ing!"

Now I recognized the large portrait that stood on the wall behind his desk, subtly shadowed in black and white: Julian Abele! There were other interesting folks on the walls of his office and books stacked to the ceiling; a fetching ladder, wheels on the bottom, gave access to the uppermost books. Sterling Brown, Charles Houston—Malcolm X and Dr. King stood on walls opposite each other—the second time I had wondered about their placement. I had much to learn about the dynamic that electrified their hunt for full citizenship.

"Caleb," Dean said, "you seem to lurch and lean like a sailor when you see those two portraits in particular. Let me tell you a story about why I have Martin and Malcolm facing each other. Anyone who has read *The Crisis of the Negro Intellectual* goes forth from Cruse's analysis with a clearer understanding of the wide avenue of choices our ancestors made in their journey toward full humanity, usually constrained by the West." Davenport tugged at his polka-dot bow tie, stretched his neck. "Through their sufferings and joys, they considered uprisings and prayer, separation and integration, nationalism and humanism. Those choices have *always* been there, a swing and sway between both men, like a pendulum pumping the hearts of individuals and groups.

"I heard both Martin and Malcolm speak over at State, as a young student from Brownsville, Tennessee. Both there in Michigan: tall shoulders! And both extremes are still important in accomplishing, fulfilling our destinies here in this country; and our destinies will all be different individually and mutually. Think about Toni Morrison—you haven't seen her because she faces me here on my desk. She added our own special survival magic to it, so that we—you, Maestro Tumbleweed—can add your story to the African American saga, just as Julian Abele did!"

I had hoped he hadn't seen that newspaper picture, and now I knew he had. Small beads of sweat broke out on my forehead. Hands clammy, I sank deep into my chair, embarrassed to my very core. "I don't know why she did that," I said in a voice both weak and feeble. A tear crawled down my cheek, and I wiped it away. "It was sooo embarrassing," I said, dismayed and crushed by the weight of things.

"I know," said Dean Davenport, "but that sort of thing happens when you least expect it; when it compounds your current pressures. But you recover, you become more resilient, you propel yourself forward, just as you have done before. Each of your instructors—I've checked with all of them—say your recent work is spectacular! Love is important, basic, and plays its part. But unless you can at the very least support yourself—which is a challenging feat in a capitalistic society, and even more so for a black man in this profession—do not neglect any opportunity to thoroughly prepare yourself. That is the best advice I can give you. I apologize for being blunt. Take that Tumbleweed picture and use it to remind you of what your next steps are. Use it as your second talisman, li'l brother." He handed me the cutout article and said, "That was one helluva dragon!"

To my surprise, we both cracked up laughing loud and long. In my mind's eye, I saw Jesse again, pipe in hand, his gold watch swinging back and forth, talking about how proud he was.

"So, Caleb, congratulations on the externship. Here are the particulars, dates, and such. They all speak English, but you might take a basic course in Greek—maybe get one of those phone apps, nothing real stressful—just so you can get around. Keep your head to the grindstone, son—to the grindstone. Read as much as you can about Abele, hand copy some of his drawings, transpose those to different times of day, night too, upside down, with both hands—right and left. Be that Chinese dragon and *breathe fire* into those exercises. Julian never got to sign his name on his work; Trumbauer signed. And Abele worked on anyway, amazing fortitude and talent. You too can *own* the shadows!"

I shook hands with the dean and thanked him, picked up the award letter and article, and thanked Ms. Arabelle for her help. "Better known as Rumbleweed," she said giving me a big hug. She

JAMES GHOLSON, JR.

watched as I put on my Civil War Antietam slouch hat—another mainstay of my incognito dress attire, and slipped on my shades, shooting her a toothy grin.

"Think reckless endangerment if you had pulled that stunt," said Arabelle, "held that water hose and tested your young lady's balance!"

"I forgot to give you another cigar," said the dean, now at the door.

Arabelle took it from him saying, "Virginia Woolf," and hooted a bark.

Vigor fueled my stride as I left the building. Heading for the sidewalk, I heard someone say, "Don't see you around much anymore, 'Weed. You still be Caleb, right?"

Heat from my spinning heels shot up to my knees; the dragon fire in my throat fired my words with steel. "Trevor," I said, "thought that might be you—red-eyed and high as usual. What can I do for ya?"

"Just hangin', homes, jus' hangin'... ain't no crime to hang," he said, slipping into his confidence-mein phase, shoulders sloped, voice smooth and mellow.

"Easy, Trev," I said, stepping away instinctively, fist clenched. "My life got real complicated a few days ago—right now, I *cherish* space."

"Understood, blood," he said, a low hiss buoying clammy words. "Jus' noticin' that we been missin' you at the meets, missin' you real bad—*and shit*. Remember, we be frat bros, mein, boon coons, blood in the bond and—*whatnot*," said Trevor.

I saw Samantha leaving her class in the background, headed my way with a girlfriend. Deciding against a public encounter, instinct took over. As I stepped around Trevor, my legs morphed into a superstrong gait, arms swinging, eyes sliding toward my apartment. Trevor's face froze nervously. With my breath, I etched hate on his face, etched his wretched grin in memory, and spoke, "Oatmeal-colored *farce*."

Samantha spun away from her friend and called "Caleb" as I sidestepped a roadblock sign. "I know you are angry with me," she said.

"I didn't chase you down with a water hose and throw keys at you. Call you out of your name—*homo-faggot*. Who got you to believe, and then *speak* that shit? You might as well have turned over the garbage can on me too—*make it real funky*," I said.

"Well, a man—a *real man*—would understand that a woman gets jealous when people tell her—"

"There you go with that *people* crap again," I said shaking. "People this, people that. F**K people! That shit was juvenile. We were together—intimate every night, most days too. You're telling me about gossip, innuendo—what *people* say, when you see me—touch me *real regula*r—*live and in perso*n, every day? To me, that has strong, clear messages about—"

"There *you* go overrationalizing again. I'm not you. I don't think or feel like you . . . don't react to—" Then she started to cry. Onlookers took in the scene with heads cocked in mixed modes. If embarrassment could crawl, I was a snake. Gravity harnessed embarrassment like a stallion, fisted folk close-by, and glued feet to pavement with its lasso. Tension flared, roared, and screamed, while a vortex of two held minions captive; a pincer attack on war-ravaged lovers. I held tissues out from my backpack. Sam shoved them into my chest and sprinted to some of her buddies.

I continued on my way home, angry and frustrated. No breakup is like one *in public.* I wanted to talk to someone but lacked a wizened friend.

"Caleb, Caleb," I heard, my name called by a familiar voice. "Hold on a minute. Man, lately you are always in a hurry!" I was lost in my own world by then; hermetically sealed in the scars of embarrassment, defeat—chaos. Trapped in the anguish and humiliation of a snake-dragon's day out, with me on the receiving end, tumbling down stairs into a wet, flaming funk, and roasted by a person with whom I had spent most of my time—*invested heart and soul.* I looked over my shoulder. It was Lara.

"Oh, hi, Lara," I said. "I didn't realize it was you."

"May I join you, walk along just for a few minutes?"

"I am not the best company at this moment."

"They come like that, the moments do. Lemme buy you a cup of coffee. I have some news for you."

X

Lara matched me stride for stride. "Saw you back there—couldn't miss what happened, out in broad daylight like that—I thought you handled it as well as could be expected. It's always interesting to see how couples almost slip into public violence. When it explodes in public, it seems especially focused and pathetically poignant," she said with a curious smirk on her face. "I can't say I would have handled that so gentlemanly if I were a guy."

"You done for the day?" I said, hoping to leave the scrape behind.

"Oh yes, I met with all my classes, got some lab work done, and spoke with a few students individually. Basically, I have grunt assignments and help students refine study habits and give a few spot quizzes on vocabulary. There is a lot of information to be familiar with in terms of anatomy . . . skeletal structure, musculature. It all boils down to fundamentals.

Generally, we have really strong students. To tell the truth, I almost didn't recognize you behind that hat and those shades, but you have a rather distinct bop in your stride that I remembered as you lowered your glasses. Let's go to Georgia's Chili. It's right over yonder!"

Those words put Lara in a special nonsecular category and drew out my smile. "What kinda news do you have for me?" I felt my nerves ratchet up a bit, stepped around her to shield her from traffic, and concentrated to avoid getting hit myself. For the first time, I noticed the nutty scent of her hair. We scooted inside the diner.

"You know that DNA can last for a long time, more than a million years in some cases, so we definitely will get DNA info back. Preliminary tests—in-house—suggest this skull is at least one hundred years old, and the hole in its crown has a form of old, military gunpowder around it. It does appear to be a bullet wound, so we might be dealing with a disturbed grave, a homicide. If I were you, I would find out exactly where Jesse found it. He should have reported it to the police or coroner's office or to an archaeologist. Now, there are cracks around the wound that suggest strikes with a blunt object, almost like a combat injury. Could you bring Jesse by?"

"I checked the other day to see if I had his contact

JAMES GHOLSON, JR.

information, Lara, and I don't. He is a friend of my dad's, an old family friend. He's kind of a weird guy. I'm not sure if he would feel comfortable with a ton of investigation around. I will try to dig him up—maybe call my mom." While saying this to Lara, Jesse's underground archaeological "dig" flashed in snapshots. *Has he disturbed an old cemetery or has he placed all that stuff there?*

"Caleb, there are all kinds of technological tools folks use in archeology; magnetic imaging, infrared and radiocarbon testing. I worked at an old Civil War site in Virginia last summer, and they made maps of shell casings to determine the flow of battle. The tests they are going to run on Skully will determine ethnicity, age, toxicity, and cause of death. We can probably answer most common questions about that skull, but it helps if we know as much as possible about it—him on the front end—where it was found, soil samples. What if this person was killed, or merely buried, in the church? Someone might think a grave was disturbed; if that is so, where is the rest of it?"

I scratched my head and scooped another spoonful of chili. Lara had a notebook and occasionally jotted stuff down. It was easy to trust Lara. Her questions made sense, and her style was scientific. I owned a ton of thoughts at this point, and most of them had not been shared. Thoughts on the externship, on

Julian Abele, on Samantha, on Jesse. My thoughts on Skully flitted about like swallows, unshared due to lack of trust. *I need to deconstruct some of those thoughts, bang them apart, and try to put back the pieces, just to see if they will function, reassembled, as a whole (to my benefit). The silverware is another story. That will definitely remain unshared—private capital. It'll support life in case I experience a bad turn.*

"Lara, Jesse has his reasons for giving me that skull. At the time, I didn't ask him what they were. I always see that silver dollar he gave me as a kid, his gold chain hanging out of his pocket, and the sumptuous black of his vest in the background, his immaculately tailored black suit."

"So, some of the tests suggest that Skully dates from the mid-eighteen hundreds, before Jesse was born. One colleague guesses he was shot execution style."

"I thought that would be from the back of the head," I said.

"Not always, but look—document the conversation when you talk to him," said Lara. "I gotta go now; the chili is my treat."

JAMES GHOLSON, JR.

It was 1950 when Jesse Steward disembarked his train from Atlanta at Union Station in the heart of Washington, D.C. He had boarded the train in Atlanta, Georgia, after taking a Greyhound bus from Memphis, Tennessee. Once he arrived in D.C.—where he knew no one—he immediately made his way to the post office and applied for work.

Jesse had been limited in his schooling, though he could "read and cipher," as DuBois would say. Earnest in his efforts to personify Booker T's "personal improvement," he secured lodging at a rooming house, and painstakingly raised the level of his dress, his vocabulary, his personal library, carriage, and basic hygiene. By trade, he was a barber; by imagination, he was a world traveler. Mr. Jesse Steward bought two pairs of army surplus brogans, five changes of undergarments and socks, and took a weekend job as night watchman for the Government Printing Office, and by day, he subbed at the post office. By his bed he kept a copy of *Webster's Unabridged Dictionary*. When he could, Jesse would attend church services at New Canaan Baptist Church, near the corner of sixth and H Northeast.

In his C Street brownstone—prudently purchased over many years—his bedroom held one implement of dresser drawers. Jesse kept a chain around his suitcase. Caked with District of Columbia dust, the suitcase lay perennially chained, in the recesses of his bedroom closet. Inside that suitcase were pictures of beloved family members—his mom and dad, sisters and cousins. They too had loved Jesse down through the years. The suitcase held evidence—in letters and parcel wrappings—that love waxed requited. When Mr. Steward's toes touched Washington pavement, he was twenty-one years old. Though he had wooed and won a number of young lovelies of the opposite sex, Jesse had never married, never produced offspring of his own, never enjoyed the hiss and bliss of marriage. Even as a child, curiosity fueled his fascination for learning, which for him occurred mainly outside the hallowed halls of ivy. Reading was his great passion, though it could not be ascertained from his speech. After fifty years in D.C., he owned that C Street brownstone, two rental properties, a lower-level library, and had sponsored several college graduates.

"Sure was glad dat Caleb stopped by today," Jesse mumbled to himself. "Ain't gots no chirren of my own, but I takes right kindly to dem kids what minds dey parents, gits dey lessons, shows adults some respect. Now dat boy gon' make sumpthin' of hisself, yessiree. Gon' be an architect, pure and simple, bettern' old Frank Lloyd." When challenged regarding his perceptions of what could be accomplished by kids of color, he was known to say, "Hell, ain't nuthin' anybody else kin do that dey can't do—fact is, I can't remember when dey evah stopped provin' it, lessen' dey had no schoolin' whatsoevah."

Jesse reached up in the cupboard to fetch a cup and pulled a pint of Old Grandad from the refrigerator. *Good kid and developing at his own pace; might have a challenge or two getting started, but that's to be expected. Silverware should hep some!* He made himself a cocktail of Old Grandad and cranberry juice, pulled up a chair, and carefully seated himself. He was careful lately because he had once missed that chair, bruised his butt, and toppled the table trying to get up. *His old daddy was a good friend and someone you could trust.* "Trustworthy," he said, bringing the cup to his lips.

Being an old farm boy, Jesse had walked behind a mule or two, plowed garden rows, and shoveled shitloads of dirt. He loved the smell of good, rich dirt and reveled in that smell in the loamy, multileveled "dig" which he cultivated at New Canaan. Nobody came down to harass or nag him. They found the steps an unnecessary hazard to "Jesse-questions," something to be avoided. In short, it was his ultimate sanctuary replete with the outdoor smells of home. He hadn't returned to Memphis since he left, but his basement "dig" helped him to remember Southern climes. The climb back up to the outside was becoming more of a physical challenge for him. Once, it had taken him two hours to reach the exit. *Couldn't bring that suitcase all de way up if'n my life depended on't—had dat skull all covered up deep, but dem rats be tryin' to get at it.*

When he left Memphis, his granny had given him clear instructions on how to handle the strange heirloom that had haunted the family since the days of the Civil War. He could still hear her say to him—in her own way both comical and deadly serious—"Take dis suitcase wid you, and when you done arrived, you point dis here skull to de North Star, *nebba, evah on slave soil—gots to be up North, on free soil!* Dat be de dream ... dem boys be *issue-free!*"

For "*mor'n a minute,*" he had that promise kept—but rodents had come to destroy his peace. Now the whole business was out of his hands. He thought he would experience relief, yet the silverware, instead of being Caleb's economic brace against the future, might be considered a bribe. What if the police considered Caleb a murderer or grave robber? "*To Canaan, to Canaan, the Lord has brought us forth;*" he recited the words to the hymn to assist him in the climb up the flights of stairs. The words helped to take his mind off the arthritis freezing his bones, hampering his climb. "*What flag is this you carry, Along the sea and shore? The same our grand-sires lifted up, The same our fathers bore.*

JAMES GHOLSON, JR.

In many a battle's tempest, It shed the crimson rain, What God has woven in his loom . . ."

———◈———

"Hi, son, is everything okay?" said Caleb's mom. "It's nice to hear from you. You caught me just as I was going to bed. You sound good."

"You too, Mom," said Caleb. "Look, I got a quick question for you."

"Oh, Caleb, we had a little row in the dining hall tonight. Some of my fellow residents showed me a picture, a newspaper clipping that was in the newspaper of a student at Harrison. One or two thought it might be you in the picture! Said they might be referring to you as *Tumbleweed* or some such thing."

"Oh no, Mom, that was another fraternity"—*hate to lie to my own mother*—"somebody else, Mom, but school officials have all that figured out now," said Caleb.

"Said that the poor fellow fell down the steps and broke his leg. Are you hurt?"

"Mom, that happened weeks ago, and, no, I'm fine," said Caleb, trying to calm her down, not wishing to cause her worry. "Look, Mom, I need a big favor."

"I know that you would have called me if you were hurt, Caleb. Your dad always said that you had grown into a responsible young man—and Jesse said the exact same thing the last time I saw him—'that boy of yours gon' be a fine architect one day, Minnie—yes'm, fine!'"

Thank God, thought Caleb. "Mom, Jesse is the reason I'm calling you. The reason I'm calling you is Jesse—do you have a phone number for him?"

"For Jesse? Um, I can look for it, but I don't think so, Caleb. Your dad always called Jesse, I never called him. But I will look through some of your dad's old books."

"Okay, and, Mom, that externship came through, so I'll be in Greece this summer."

"Wonderful, son, just wonderful. You will enjoy that. Be sure to give me the dates."

"I will, Mom. Get your rest now. I'm not going to talk long and call me if you find a number for Jesse. I'll call the church and check with them. Love you, Mom; will you call again soon."

It was only *after* Mom hung up that I remembered my namesake, Granduncle Caleb, who had been killed in World War I, and my uncle Thomas, buried alive in World War II. Abele's career had bloomed *between* two world wars. My own skeleton rattled on that thought. What a wonderful piece of luck for him!

XI

My thoughts bubbled with questions as I got off the subway at Union Station. With me I had two photos of Skully, found in Jesse's suitcase, the blueprint, and sketch Davenport had given me, my cell phone, pencils and paper, all sandwiched into my backpack. Tourists around the place skipped and skirted the whereabouts on Segway personal transporters. I noticed the angle of their forward leans, amused that they resembled the angle of my precipitous stairway descent. The jangle of my phone alerted me to an incoming call. "Hullo," I said, eyes focused on the Beaux Arts sprawl of Union Station itself. I had risen early, first to catch Jesse, and then visit an off campus library, preferably the old Carnegie on H Street to research Julian Abele.

"You up?" said Samantha, hearing traffic in the background.

"Rollin', whassup?"

"Spring break is almost here. I remembered we chatted about a quick getaway. What's that noise? Are you outside?"

"Downtown headed to church; tryin' to catch Jesse, and then spend sometime in the library on H Street. Yeah, I remember—that was before—"

"So, sounds like you are busy. Anyway, just thought I would check. You said you could help me with this math, but Trevor said he's had the course."

"Gotta go, Samantha. He sounds like a decent choice. We'll talk." Nerves edgy, I felt immediately jangled and forced myself back into my initial stride. *Trevor this, Trevor that. Substitutes wear thin if that's the game.* As I rounded the corner at Sixth and H Northeast, I stopped to take several photos of the church.

"My architect!" sounded from the half-opened door in Jesse's deep baritone voice. "Twice in the same month? You're setting a record," said Jesse. "Went down into my dungeon digs yesterday and almost couldn't get back up all dem steps. Arthur is tryin' to take me down, Caleb, tryin' to *freeze* my bones."

With architect Julian Abele at the front of his mind, Caleb's question came out like this: "Jesse, who was the architect for this building? I mean, talk about sturdy construction!"

JAMES GHOLSON, JR.

"I bes' bring out de blueprint fur that'un, Caleb. Don' rightly know. Ain't got no idea."

"The stained-glass work is really beautiful, like flowers exploding from within the Promised Land!"

"You be reapin', boy, jus' like in John 4:5–42, 'One sows, and another reaps. I sent you to reap that for which you did not labor. Others have labored, and you have entered into their labor.' Our forefathers picked all that cotton, so's you kin *choose* to become de architect, and reap dis beauty to build beauty of your own. And build it you must, Caleb, to counter evil. Germany tried to build beauty, Caleb—Mozart, Beethoven, Brahms, Bach—all that beauty and Hitler grew out of it. Build good and beauty with all your might, cuz it will get challenged wid slavery and holocausts and larceny: fake dis and dat!"

"Jesse, I want you to know how much I appreciate your gifts to me. I want—"

"I knowed dat, son. You be here on account of dat skull!"

Caleb said nothing and stared at the sidewalk.

"Come on in here, boy and have some coffee and a doughnut. Glory be, son, glory be. Dat skull reminded me many times of de Capitol Dome—milky, cheese-colored, luminous and full. A half-mooned, medieval helmet with a tint of steel on it now and agin'. Holds the brains, and de brains makes imagination. Might have to ask Pastor for blueprints." Jesse entered the building, opened the janitor's closet, poured coffee and coffee fixins', and procured two doughnuts, "One fur you, one fur Jesse." Jesse crossed himself.

Caleb punched the recording app on his cell phone.

"Lak I said, I brought alla dat stuff to D.C. wid me in fifty. Parked it underneath my bed at first, then buried it here, jus' in case. Wanted to be sure it be buried in de *Promised Land up North,* like Granny said—in her own way—'Boy, you take allus dis wid you, 'specially dis here skull—dis boy needs be buried *issue-free* in free soil—so's he kin look back at de South and spit if'n he gits good and ready!' Dats what she say, yessir! Brought it all, mostly, from Memphis, polished at de time; candelabras, shakers for salt and pepper, forks, spoons, knives, bowls, serving dishes, pistol. Jesse done what he could wid dat skull. If some authority ax you where it come from, you say, 'Jesse brought it to D.C. from Memphis in a gunny sack.'" Jesse repeated himself, slower, head upturned, sotto voce, *"Dis boy needs be buried issue-free—'cuz he ain't no slave—in free soil, so's he kin look back at de South and spit if'n he gits good and ready!"*

They both sat in silence for more than a minute, Jesse lost in the past, Caleb in the future 'til Jesse started singing, *"To Canaan, to Canaan, de Lord has*

JAMES GHOLSON, JR.

led us forth, to blow b'fo' the heathen walls de trumpets of de North!"

"Now dat stuff been in de fam'ly since Civil War days, since the bell rung. De skull come from dose days, I reckon; can't say fur sure. Black folk closer to it despised dose times, said one thing, meant another. Spoke so as to be understood only by those dey trusted. Trust may run in colors but is defined by character, like water. Now, this is partly rumor, but after dem battles, who'd you think buried dem bodies, dug dem holes, sweated in de sun, son? *Generals?* Jackson, Nashville, Shiloh, Chickamauga. Rebs had blacks wid um as body protectors—*were still slaves, mind ya*—posted on grave-digger detail. And black men were signing up for duty with the Union so's to gain freedom, thanks to Mr. Lincoln. But I can't say for sure where that skull comes from. I jus' followed Granny's wishes, pure an' simple. What I kin say for sure is dat as soldiers, de black soldier got de gun afore education, so de gun was de government's first step. Look around at de rates of readin', education for urban black folk. You might conclude dat ain't nothin' changed."

Lara had guessed right on the time frame, and I had testimony from Jesse now on his memories. I would transcribe the MP3 and add written notes to satisfy any need for documentation. Jesse hadn't got mad with me for raising these questions with him. The last thing I wanted was for him to think me ungrateful, and I knew more about his family, sisters, and Grandma than I had known previously.

"I know that you appreciate the silver," said Jesse, "but, Caleb—I'm getting old, and if you find dat skull a burden, den you jus' bury it right alongside wid me when de time comes. I'll count on you fur dat!"

In many ways, Skully was still a mystery; so was the architect of New Canaan. I gave Jesse a bro-hug and headed for the old D.C. Library on H Street, formerly known as the Carnegie Public Library. It now houses the Historical Society. Incognito, I wanted to more thoroughly check out Julian Abele. I hooked a ride via Uber and sent Lara a text . . . "Just interviewed Jesse, more later."

The Carnegie Library at Mount Vernon Square has long been one of my favorite places. It possesses an aura of elegance and charm that outclasses much of the steel and glass occupying the spaces around it. Dad had found it a conspicuous space of peace. I checked in, asked for and received permission, and began to experiment with a few ideas Davenport had given me. I sketched bookcases in window light, tracking beams of indoor splendor, shadows of desks, and arcs of windows using both hands and repeating the best sketches from new times and vantage points. At intervals of fifteen minutes, I researched the life of Julian Abele, tracking youthful development in Philadelphia. Then I began work on copying the blueprints Davenport gave me. Four o'clock rolled around. Outside, a solo saxophonist serenaded a large crowd of rapt listeners, shoppers, pedestrians, and tourists. It was a beautiful and colorful sight. I stopped to inhale the music and fresh air; the performer utterly ensconced in riffs, arpeggios, vivid melodies and bebop rhythms. His audience was completely spellbound, and I was reminded of Sonny Rollins.

"Stop! Put it back or pay for it! Stop, thief, thief—stop him!" The strident scream of a chubby merchant broke the spell of the musical magician and drew attention to a specter of bright tennis shoes and a white baseball cap, weaving its way through pedestrians scattering like newly wakened cockroaches. I had just crossed to the bus stop, boarding the bus on a wave of panicked pedestrians. *Gotta leave these crowds alone* very briefly crossed my mind.

Bang! Bang! Bang! rang out in a flurry of shots. The bus filled in seconds with screaming, panicked persons from all directions. I hit the deck immediately, just as the window above me was shattered. Not only did glass spray all over the place, but I ended up covered by almost five layers of townsfolk. Luckily,

I still clutched my backpack as if life itself resided within it.

Eventually, a commanding woman's voice ordered us to a new bus. "Ladies and Gentlemen, this is a crime scene. Please exit carefully to the bus in front of us." The tall policewoman quietly oversaw, first the exit, and then the boarding of our new vehicle. In between exiting and boarding, passengers from our buses gawked and hissed at the young black man, now handcuffed in the back of a police car. I was happy to be on the move.

Once home, I raided the fridge for food, finding leftover pizza and soft drinks. I nuked the pizza and studied the sky outside, glad that I had reached my apartment in one piece. In the distance, I noticed shards of lightning strike the ground, highlighting the Capitol Dome. I heard no thunder, just flashes of resplendent light. Seated after several deep breaths, I found myself floating backward through my travels of the day and closed my eyes to reimagine conversation with Jesse and spied on myself copying Abele's drawings.

BOOM, boom, ka-boom! Thunderclaps sounded after sparks orbited a radio tower in the far distance and closer by—right outside my window—I heard the soft pitter-patter of raindrops, globs of raindrops, soft like miniature feathers. Jagged shards of lightning bore me air-bound like crutches, and I lumbered on lightning stilts, back down Georgia Avenue. Nope, I don't think so, I said to the policewoman as she stopped traffic to allow me first to cross the street, and then to continue back to the library—back past the point where shots occurred.

She pointed to the young, hooded man they had in the back of the police vehicle. "Is he the one?" she said. I looked away from the fellow, not wanting to get involved, not wanting to witness.

Bars of lightning flashed again. I was in a *jail* of lightning, of flashing lightning. I saw Jesse, seated inside his janitor's closet, in a *policeman's* uniform. *"Dis boy needs be buried issue-free in free soil—so's he kin look back at de South and spit if'n he gits good and ready!"* said Jesse, as if making me witness Skully's anguish at the questions I'd asked. *"Den you jus' bury it right alongside wid me when de time comes!"* I watched myself hear those words, watched a tear roll down my cheek, and saw me double over shamefully, happy to receive shiny pieces of silver, but reluctant to bear the burden of burial, burial of a freeman in free soil. Then I was on those crutches again, they had grown now—giant, oversized stilts—and I used them like pencils to draw replicas of Abele's sketches in the Reflecting Pool down by the Washington Memorial.

Boom, boom, ba-boom! Brilliant, luminous flashes

of lightning spiked the head of that dragon in the Potomac River and spotlit the Lincoln Memorial as if it were a stage with no curtains! My stilts grew taller and for unknown and baffling reasons, I found myself airborne—not blocking any flight patterns at the airport—just floating in cold, rainy somersaults, headed in no particular direction. *Gravity-less, above the Capitol's crown, above the nation's capital, and I am freezing! To skim, skate, spin, and frolic in the moonlit beams above the Capitol Dome is an experience unlike any other. Transcendent and cold, I yelled, "FREEZING!" as loudly as possible, in my most strident voice, but there was no sound. WEIRD! I looked for icicles, looked down at the dome on the building—rounded, sleek, holder of American brains, voice of the people—elocutionists of imagination—there was the campus far off in the distance to the northeast.*

Captured by ever-stronger gusts of wind, I found myself rinsed wet by torrents of windblown rain and captured by chilling waterfalls down toward the Capitol Dome! Yikes! I tried breaking my skid, but catapulted, rising into the air again . . . like I was on a slide-board, and tossed airborne. My lips and neck shivered! In the southeast, I saw the radio tower tumble, over and over, almost as if it were a—a KEY! Yes, a silver key! It was the same metallic color of an airplane . . . ALUMINUM! I saw myself, high above that dome, sliding down a frozen

JAMES GHOLSON, JR.

snowdrift, tumbling head over heels, reaching for—my key. Oh boy! I was most amazed that I had yet to break anything or feel pain. Several times, after riding crests of waterfalls, I tried to break my fall, change my slope or incline, but no matter what I did—kick my feet, wave my arms, yell, scream, swim—nothing changed my course of direction or the course of events around me. I tobogganed into infinity. The last time I zoomed downward, I saw it—red-tongued, fire exhaling, wide-mouthed—THE DRAGON—reach up out of the brackish Potomac and lurch—open-throated, red-tongued, and gloriously venomous—to find raw meat—to lash me, on my backside.

My drop, duck, and roll landed me on the floor of my apartment! Awake immediately, I felt the wetness of the back and collar of my shirt. The sofa pillow was wringing wet.

"You better get in the bed," I told myself and checked the door locks before turning in. I wrote on an index card—s*ee Abele*—and headed for bed. It had been a *very* long day.

XII

The photos and sketches I'd downloaded, architectural images and concept drawings of art and architecture created by Julian Abele threw me into fits ranging from fascination to reverie. I was captivated—no—ensorcelled—by his remarkable mastery. Each image sizzled with a pernicious incandescence of talent, regardless of medium. Whether it was a village church, the Conklin Gate Exedra, the Duke Chapel, or library, they floated, mesmerized, enchanted, and defied easy reduction to a simple technique: *they mystified*. I had studied them a bit on my way to the train station. I was headed to Duke to see his work, both physically and conceptually, for myself.

The dream I'd experienced a few days ago forced a recalculation, kept me on a trajectory to raise the bar of my academics, sustain a higher caliber of work, prepare for my trip to Greece, and whip anxieties which were freezing my self-confidence in place. I'd e-mailed both the MP3 of Jesse's and my transcription of that interview to Lara, financially secured the safe-deposit box of silverware, and learned a little more about Skully. There still remained a tincture of embarrassment on my "Tumbleweed" moment. My humbled soul and Antietam slouch hat and dark glasses kept me secretly cloaked and comfortable. Abele's Conklin Exedra—an entryway for conversation and discussion—stimulated my thinking about Samantha, about the strengths and weaknesses of our rapport, and reflecting on what might be next steps.

Defined as a place of conversation, an exedra is often semicircular in shape and with a solid back. I was unsure of when and where that conversation would take place and felt relief that I would have some time to gain a new perspective on our dilemma. My research on Abele led me to an important discovery: Abele had taught himself to draw with his off-hand (left) because he feared loss of his right hand would end his career. I thought of my basketball player friends who knew that effectiveness with both hands, dribbling-wise, is expected as a skill in the twenty-first century. Abele used this fear as a means of inspiring himself to become more competent. I committed to duplicating his success in myself. Davenport had sent me an emoji during one of my classes—trigonometry, I think—after I had dropped off one of my left-handed copies ... An acknowledgment that he was somewhat pleased with my meager attempts.

Still, I wondered about what had ticked off Samantha and thought about it on the Thursday before spring break, wondering about this on my various trips about campus. Had someone injected a misconception—a rumor or innuendo—about my carrying boxes with Lara? Had someone reported us chatting, that might have gotten under her skin that I didn't know about? I gave this consideration on and off. The one thing that infuriated me was her public gesture, without her discussing her anger with me. The timing, plus the capture of my fall on the front page of the papers, was almost as if the whole thing had been staged—a setup. Her anger had revealed a crack in our rapport that diminished my ability—our ability—to communicate, to care for each other, to integrate our thoughts as a unit. What would the future hold when other, more emergent challenges would come our way? Would she attack me even more fiercely in the wake of new rumors or innuendos? As the train moved southward through Northern Virginia, I decided to wish her a pleasant break and sent her one of my favorite sonnets, by Shakespeare, one that I had read in lit class a few years ago.

JAMES GHOLSON, JR.

> *No more be grieved at that which thou hast done:*
> *Roses have thorns, and silver fountains mud:*
> *Clouds and eclipses stain both moon and sun,*
> *And loathsome canker lives in sweetest bud.*
> *All men make faults, and even I in this,*
> *Authorizing thy trespass with compare,*
> *Myself corrupting, salving thy amiss,*
> *Excusing thy sins more than thy sins are;*
> *For to thy sensual fault I bring in sense,*
> *Thy adverse party is thy advocate,*
> *And 'gainst myself a lawful plea commence:*
> *Such civil war is in my love and hate,*
> *That I an accessory needs must be,*
> *To that sweet thief which sourly robs from me.*

Sad as it was, it captured the mood I was in and held a muted apology that captured the mental confusion I felt, an abiding appreciation and love still present in my heart. What stood in my way? I tried to put the whole mess out of my mind. My reflections took a new turn, one which centered on black fraternities and sororities that existed on campus. Away from home and keyed into studies in a new environment, the Greek system of engaging new friends, integrating new personalities and customs from different parts of the country—indeed, the world—held a deep interest to me. Our frat house bull sessions, parties, chess and card games were fun. I knew that many of the individuals I hung out with would be lifelong friends. The system also familiarized initiates with hierarchies of social status, much like boarding and military schools. We talked endlessly about politics, art, philosophy, classes, and very actively about mentors, male and female archetypes—those who were helping and guiding us into chosen professions; how we would be similar and how different. And we came from an amazing assortment of backgrounds.

Now, approaching my fifth year in architectural design, I had incorporated a few crucial study and reading habits I'd learned from these friends. Polishing these skills was important, as Harrison was a truly competitive academic environment. Being challenged and challenging fellow students regarding belief systems fueled bull sessions, often lasting deep into the night. Most of us had not attended boarding schools or military academies. Some, like Trevor, were products of those environments, prolific in social grace, stumblers in loyalty. Perhaps an avenue suggesting physical retaliation or psychological belittlement as consequences for missteps on the part of pledges. Weren't these the tools of slavery?

As the train approached Richmond, I decided to make a quick run to the head and grab a hot dog and coffee. The conductor sang out, "Richmond!

JAMES GHOLSON, JR.

Richmond, Virginia." I sallied to the condiments car, paid for my order, and headed back to my seat.

"Hey, mister," said a four- or five-year-old kid sporting a cowboy hat and the words *Buffalo Soldier* across the chest of a bright, yellow shirt. "I'm a buffalo soldier."

"You sure are," I said, "kinda sharp too. I used to have a hat like that."

"Sir," said the woman sitting beside him, "could you hand me two of those pillows on the upper rack?"

"Can do," I said and promptly handed two pillows to the woman I assumed to be his mother. They sat in the row of seats just in front of mine.

"Did you ever ride a buffalo?" said the youngster.

"Nope," I said, with a big smile on my face, "but I drove one once upon a time."

"No, you didn't," he said, eyes bulging. "You can't drive a buffalo!"

"Yes, you can," I said laughing. "All you have to do is put a steering wheel on it."

The wheels in his eyes really started churning then. "Mommy, that man tells stories. Is there such a thing as a wheel for a buffalo?"

His mother gave me a pretty smile and settled him down for a while. Occasionally, he would look back at me through the armrest-space between the seats. Gradually, the rhythm of the wheels on the tracks helped me calibrate my way back to my thoughts on Samantha, on Greek life, and, of course, on my upcoming trip to Greece. What would I find, and what would I learn there? I'd heard of Bernard Tschumi in one of my classes. Thumbing through architecture journals, I'd seen some of his videotapes on YouTube and knew him to head the team of architects that built the New Acropolis Museum. I rewrote this handwritten ditty, remembering its lilt, but unsure of where it originally came from:

> *Whose walls are these you're smashing,*
> *With timbrel, song, and tongue,*
> *Can Canaan's corpus raising,*
> *Be dubbed the Abele Run?*

Thankfully, this trip would take most of the night with me arriving early in Durham at 6:50 a.m. The thought of tracking down whomever was playing mind games with Samantha beckoned; it would take both time and energy. Right now, both came to me at a premium, though I have always been excited by the chase for truth. Rocking forth on this train was part of that chase, just as a patient rummage through campus social orbits might ferret out those fake gossip and psychic constructs aimed at us both. On my phone I sent e-mail messages to my professors explaining my absence from Friday's classes. I then reread biographical notes on Julian Abele; his children, marriage, education at the Colored Institute in Philadelphia (eventually becoming Cheney State), his love of the Philadelphia Orchestra, and his employment by Harold Trumbauer. Occasionally, I would look backward to see the tail of the train slither right or snake left.

"Hey, mister," said my little friend again, peeping around to see me, "my name is Zach. What's yours?"

"Caleb," I said.

"Wanna see my pillow-fort? All buffalo soldiers have pillow-forts, even when they are out on the range," Zach said. He pointed to the collection of blankets, pillows, and his backpack, all very admirably constructed to provide . . . "protections from bandits and outlaws," he said for my edification. He'd added his mom's umbrella for a center pole, as she had fallen into a grateful snooze. "Tomorrow, I'll show you the ramparts. Mom is snoozing on them now."

I put my finger to my lips and whispered, "Yep, you have a pretty mom, and she might be kinda tired. If I were you, I would let her grab some shut-eye, partner. We'll get pictures for the newspaper in the morning," I said.

"The newspaper!" said Zach, "Oh boy, Mom, he's a *newspaper* man." Once again, my cleverness had backfired.

His mom fish-eyed me, smiled, and said, "Zach, you are going to be on my knee in two seconds if you don't go to sleep. That man is doing his homework."

"Good night, Mr. Caleb," said Zach.

"Night, Zach," I said.

I was especially keen to see as many original versions of Abele's work as I could get my hands on. Abele had a saying, often quoted in various texts I perused, "The lines may be those of Horace Trumbauer, but the *shadows* are all mine." I liked that phrase and found his techniques for shading and shadowing to be remarkable, adding buoyancy and effervescence to his sketches and drawings. Abele, pronounced, "Able," was a nickname by his collegiate schoolmates "Ready, Willing, and Able." I enjoyed reading about his development. Pictures taken later in his life showed him to be, in my eyes, a very disciplined person. I read for a bit more, fought sleep with another run to get coffee and plain cake, revisited the lavatory, and went to sleep wondering about those constraints of the Jim Crow era. *Couldn't even sign his name to his drawings! Damn.*

XIII

"Hey, sir, steppin' high off dat train, ain't cha?" The woman's voice was high, strained, strident. "Kin you spare dis here old lady a dollar or two?" I had just cleared the Durham station and was on my way to catch a cab, 7:15 a.m.

"Hi," I said. "I only have a dollar to spare. Here you can have—"

"Cheap muthfsucker!" and the begging greeter snatched the bill and ambled away.

Once seated inside the Duke Library and properly registered as a student from another institution, I put in motion my observation/sketch plan. I had already downloaded the images I wanted to copy; however, I wanted to see those preconstruction drawings live. "Is it possible to see the architectural drawings of Julian Abele for the library, live?" I asked the librarian.

"Oh yes," responded the librarian, "but you cannot

take photos of the material. They are on display for public use."

Immediately I walked over to the display materials and studied the drawings, taking mental notes of the clear technical details and reclaimed my seat after a short time. I also noted sketches of the chapel and several other campus buildings. I made hand sketches of each drawing, turning my computer images by degrees—ninety degrees, one hundred and eighty degrees, two hundred and seventy degrees—to challenge my powers of observation and accuracy, see if I could come close to the level of clarity and accurateness contained in these drawings. Fully aware that my efforts would render themselves comic caricatures, at times pitiful, I persisted with dogged commitment, recording what I saw faithfully.

As a break from my renderings, I took occasional walks on the premises, gradually allowing my musings to grow bolder. I wandered about Abele's papers, minor drawings, sketches, and construction photos in an attempt to harness and understand the serpentine relationship he maintained with the developers of Duke's West Campus. How could he manage the project from Philadelphia? His talent was indeed in the shadows, as was his humanity. But I witnessed his immense devotion to each step of architectural artistry, first in concept drawings, then in organic

JAMES GHOLSON, JR.

blueprints, and in the final product—envisioned and refined by an intercontinental, applied apprenticeship—in photos. The markings on these papers were successive instances of genius, constrained by Jim Crow stupidity, but not enfeebled by its physical or psychic hobbles. I walked back to the exhibit to read snippets of documentation on the life of Mr. Abele.

Julian Abele was born into a respected African American family. His father, Charles Abele, was born a freedman in Chester, Pennsylvania, in 1841. He fought for the Union, was wounded, and eventually settled in nearby Philadelphia, where he worked as a laborer at the U.S. Treasury Customs House, a coveted patronage position. Julian's mother, Mary Jones Abele, was a milliner and collateral descendant of Absalom Jones, the first rector of the African Church of Philadelphia. Julian graduated in 1897 from Philadelphia's acclaimed Institute for Colored Youth (ICY), founded by the Society of Friends of Quakers in 1852. There, his aunt Julia Jones taught drawing and steered him toward a career in architecture. In 1898, he earned a Certificate in Architectural Design from the Pennsylvania Museum and School of Industrial Arts. In 1902, Abele graduated from the School of Architecture, the University of Pennsylvania, and in 1903, he received a Certificate of Completion in Architectural Design from the

Pennsylvania Academy of Fine Arts. In the latter three institutions, Abele was the first of his race to earn a certificate or degree.

Back at my desk, I reflected a bit on my quick breakfast at the student center, my brisk photo-taking walk toward the library, and leafed through earlier photos on my smartphone. Perhaps I should take photos of some of these buildings at various times of day—sketching those photos and capturing changes in light, color, and atmosphere would give me a good bit of challenging practice. Before following through on that, I studied one large image of the interior of Duke Chapel, a grand ship tilted upside down. The shadows and detail of this image literally jumped off the page: the silent grandeur of the ribbed arches, sculptured windows appearing manifestly touchable—embossed. Taken as a whole, the drawing was sublimely spectacular, making me feel surrounded, swaddled, and celebrated in a divine presence.

What would happen if I sketched in shadows first, before unique items, vary the intensity of the shadows, and force them alive with grays and blacks and in-betweens? Even in shadows, light pulsates. I decided to vary my vantage points, to surround my subjects—play the part of an airborne drone with pincerlike movements—and photograph them in sequence as if I were a military historian.

JAMES GHOLSON, JR.

Outside, I wandered for a bit in the Quad considering the way Abele incorporated historical precedence—the Beaux Arts conventions—into buildings designed for the contours of Duke's campus. In every direction, there were themes, counterthemes, and rhythmic revelations in archways, flying buttresses, wrought-iron touches, the use of Hillsborough stone for the buildings. I am *tracking* you, Mr. Abele. I want to learn your secrets!

In my stroll about campus, an incendiary love and passion for the art of architecture took hold, seizing my spirit and imagination: I felt Abele speak to me: behold the possible!

"Look at what you did in spite of Jim Crow constraints, in spite of segregated schools, in spite of your name lurking in the shadows. Magnificent," I murmured, "Oh . . ." and smiled, remembering Zach in his pillow-fort. Surely Abele had asked his dad if he'd seen a fort in the Civil War, if his dad could describe a rampart, gun turret, or bombproof. *Trumbauer had recognized your talent and supported your study in Europe—Paris and Greece.* I stepped back inside, further perusing the exhibit.

Another snippet read, *"Most clients, however, never realized that Abele was chief designer; and due to his race, his name was not well-known outside of Philadelphia architectural circles until after Trumbauer's death."* Nonetheless, his friends in Philadelphia vividly remember his personality and taste: *"He drew with unmatched facility and worked in many mediums: water color, lithography, etching, pencil; in wood, iron, gold, silver. Abele designed all his own furniture and made it, even doing the petit point himself. While he knew many historic styles, he seemed to love Louis XIV French most of all . . . He was conscious of good architecture everywhere and very careful to relate his buildings to what was around them."* (Henry Magaziner, "As I Remember Julian Abele")

I had settled back into my seat and resumed my copy work, this time using my left hand, when my phoned chimed, loudly sounding forth its version of The Commodores', "Brick House," and drawing the unmistakable ire of patrons at nearby desks. Belatedly, after much fumbling and punching, I silenced it and got back to work.

"Sir," said the librarian in tones of contrived patronage, "glad to see you got your phone off. Hey, that's pretty good! Are you an artist?"

I apologized for the intrusion and said, "Well, I am working on becoming one of sorts. I am really enjoying your exhibit of these materials of Abele's." She smiled and demurred, leaving me to reexamine my little offender.

I noticed a text sent to me by Lara. "Skully

seems to have cleared any legal issues that could come his way; the coroner attests to him not being recent. Forensic results indicate that he's almost one hundred and fifty . . . as of 2014 . . . died of a gunshot wound to the head. Will save documents for you and hope all is well. Saw Samantha on campus yesterday—she struts well—wearing a coal miner's hat! Call me," Lara.

I responded with, "Trip very inspiring—all good. Finding good stuff on Abele and a treat to see Duke campus."

I gathered my pencils, pen, and erasers, tossed everything into my backpack, and headed outside. At the desk I asked if there was a good restaurant nearby. "Coal Miner's Daughter," was one of Samantha's favorites, and, amused by Lara's observation, slipped into the song. I wondered if the tune was Sam's antistress agent. Once outside, I texted her again. "Yeah, used to wear that thing around the crib a lot; but never saw her underneath it on campus; she's from West Virginia!" When I looked up from my phone, I noticed a team of groundskeepers who fish-eyed me, dropped their gaze, and returned to the repair and pruning work absorbing their attention—mostly. I was in the mood for biscuits and some scrambled eggs. "Mornin," I said, "hate to disturb you gentlemen, but can you tell me the best place to get some

North Carolina biscuits and scrambled eggs?" They broke into peals of laughter.

The supervisor among them was a rather elderly gentleman of a deep walnut complexion. "Mornin', sonny," he said blowing a steady puff of blue smoke from his pipe into the air. "Ain't seed you 'round these parts afore. Figured you be from up North somewheres." His eyes slowly evaluated my dress and face, while his quick sideways glance hurled the others back into their cutting and hammering. "North Carolina biscuits?" he said, giving the term his full attention. "Those biscuits be animate or inanimate?"

For more than a minute, I couldn't figure out exactly what he was talking about. Then I heard another round of laughter lurk around my question and finally said, "I don't have a girlfriend in these parts—inanimate would best describe my question."

"Got jus' the place for you, den; right over yonder gots the best of both in town. What brings you to town?" he said.

I studied the white of his beard and hair, trying not to be cross at the slow tempo in which he scrutinized my words.

"Well, I came down from D.C. to use the library and examine the work of Julian Abele. I'm finishing up my degree in architecture at Harrison and jus' learned of his architectural contributions."

JAMES GHOLSON, JR.

He responded more quickly, then, and said, "Young pups 'bout campus still don' know all that much. Man was a genius mor'n five times the worth of dese here 'temporary' critters. Seen you in de library earlier, drawin' away—draw pretty good too. Ah gits to bathe in the sunshine of ol' Abele (Able) evah day—no accent grave on dat las' 'e.' Go git you somethin' to eat . . . If you wants, Ah be happy to show you 'round a bit."

"Gimme a time," I said, anxious to see the perspective of an elder who had watched over and maintained Abele's structures—up close and personal—over the years. "Three o'clock, sonny," the old man said. "Be right cher waitin' on ya!"

XIV

3:01: I stood just outside the library entrance, my eyes glued to my cell phone, scanning for text and mail messages.

"Glory be, son, I always wanted to be an architect myself," said Lester the supervisor. During the previous two hours, I had studied pictures of the 1928 construction process which documented the building of the West Campus; the pictures recorded a paucity of African Americans. I wondered if the ratios of blacks to whites in those photos come anywhere close to the census percentages of blacks in Durham during that period. *Those photos are frozen documentation of the racial segregation of the time: generally, no black folk!*

"Hey, Lester," I said, "been looking at pics of the construction process and saw few, if any, black construction workers."

"Naw, li'l brother, you ain't 'bout to see us in those

photos and don' get me started talking on Jim Crow. Can't imagine what Abele felt 'bout that crap—had to be a very patient man to deal with de constraints of dat time. Seems to me dat Duke done finally started to grow up, honoring him right proper like they been doing. Think about it! He don' showed what a black man can do, given a chance and a supportive, *enlightened*, and humane climate. Don' surprise me one bit what he done, wid a daddy and mom like he had. I know a book about him is comin'... needs to be soon so's to inspire some of these young'uns," he said.

I said, "Yeah, I know; wish I had known about him earlier, but it's not too late."

"Man went all over Europe to fashion his trade, lookin' for relatives too—France, Germany, Italy—in de Bible too, right there with Cain and Abel. If'n he'd tried to come to school here, dey woulda hung his ass right from dat chapel. Now dey rings that bell in honor of him. *Crazy*." Lester started walking and waved for me to join him. "Mor'n I want to think about. How much longer you gonna be around?"

"Not long," I said.

I followed him into the bowels of the library. As we descended, he reached into a tall locker on the wall, slipped on a miner's hard hat, and switched on the light that guided us into the basement. Immediately, I thought of Jesse, and then pictured Samantha. *Why on earth would she traipse across campus in a coal miner's hard hat?*

Lester showed me the heating apparatus, the plumbing setups, and explained how they had put in the air-conditioning system. He shined the light on the blueprints held in his hands, and I compared them to the papers. They shook in his hands as I stared at them thinking, *I have much to learn.*

"I'm here until tomorrow."

"Great! Then we'll continue tomorrow, right after lunch. I want you to see the chapel. Abele was really inspired when he designed dat building. To me, it seems like it comes straight out of a vision from heaven. Like I said, his vision for our campus has pieces of a big ol' town square in de old country; people crisscrossing one another as dey walks about."

I rechecked my shoulder bag to make sure that I forgot nothing, made my way back to my motel, and ordered a pizza. I felt imbued with the vigor of Mr. Abele's spirit as it passed from his artistry through Lester to me. I experienced a chill in the library basement, remembering Abele's words, "*I own the shadows.*" That was a consistent characteristic that defined his work, an adept use of shadowing technique unerringly calibrated. Gradations here, cross-hatchings there, and smudges in grays and blacks. *What kind of pencils did he use?*

I sent a long text to Mom, assuring her I yet breathed, and placed a call to Lara.

"Caleb," she said, "good to hear from you. You got my message?"

"I did, and thought I might get a better feel for it by chatting face-to-face, so to speak," I said.

She laughed heartily and said, "Look, after you left, I thought I would go by the offices of the student paper, just to see what kind of photos they had of that Chinese dragon that turned up at your frat house. Guess what?"

"What?" I said.

"Photos of that incident were sent to them from all over the place. They musta had more than thirty from off campus folk and ten or eleven from students!"

"You're kidding," I said.

"Nope. And there are a few—more than one or two—that show some interesting close-ups of the *feet* in those photos; some very interesting things—on a scale of size ten, I'd say elevens or *twelves*—going on under that dragon skin. I'll show you when you get back. By the way, when are you going to get back?"

"Coming back Sunday."

"Well, call me."

"Will do," I said, "and sleep tight."

It's funny how things sometimes develop. I

reflected on my own fear of the Deep South, its emotional and *economic* darkness, its need for something called a *nigger*. My knees had trembled when Lester led the way into the bowels of the library. I feared most the historic absence of enlightenment; in my own consciousness that fear trailed me to Durham. Last night was the first time Lara and I had spoken without bringing up the subject of Skully. Did she intuit my fear of darkness and loss of imagination that came with Skully's condition? Had she witnessed the Skully in me? That was the most awesome thing about Abele; even in darkness, he found light in the shadows! Old Lester's hard hat lit our way. I came to Durham with my knees trembling, no hard hat, no *personal* light for Southern mores. Abele was here to lay down the mantle. *I'll never rest 'til you pick up the mantle and chase me for your dreams!* I hadn't dreamed since water-skiing over the Capitol Dome in a cold sweat. Now, I dreamed wide awake, as Skully mocked me dancing a ghostly *Skully-shuffle*, outfitted in a suit worthy of Hickey Freeman.

The next morning I was at the library before the doors opened. I sketched copies of the plant in its setting. Abele had sketched using pencils of varying softness, from two to nine on the HB graphite scale. I learned that in an online search. Pencils of this variety were found *outside* the United States.

JAMES GHOLSON, JR.

Abele had enjoined this European technique to deliver broad contrasts and luminosity in his work. My left hand was becoming more fluid and accurate, and I loved the additional depth and flexibility it brought to my work. I warmed up using both hands drawing straight lines. I had pencils of two different hardnesses, vowing to buy those on the HB scale soon. I experimented with pencils I had; my shadows took on more depth! I found I could play more with intermediate origins of light. Though my renditions were more accurate, I still fell a good bit short in the arena of lightness. I pressed on, though, convinced that I could master the art of light and shadows, inching my way to lightness.

I met Lester right after lunch at the Duke Library entrance.

"Hey, li'l brother," he said, greeting me with a handshake, "did ya git anything done?"

"Oh yeah, I'm getting closer to understanding his sketch technique."

The guy had a mechanic's eye for accuracy and angles, and an artist's touch for buoyancy. He was a true master. "I'm getting closer; not there yet."

"Well, at least ya know what it takes to git closer. We're headin' to Baldwin Auditorium first—jus' a drive-by—and then we spend some time at the chapel. I want you to be sure to see that chapel before you leave. Baldwin is where the concerts happen, where de classical arts and de rank and file—de common man meet, where the great glory and dis'pline of joy, 'preciatshun and study join."

I took some snapshots of the domed building. From the street it appeared recently refurbished. I could only imagine the history of sounds that had decorated that place. Before I knew it, we were at the chapel and stopped to park.

How to describe the palpitations of my heart as I approached the Duke chapel! Lester limped before me, his hard hat attached to his belt, as we approached the portal. It stood proudly before us as I said, "Lester, let me take a selfie of us. You have been very kind to take your time to make sure I see this place. I thank you for that."

"I'm happy to do it . . . Whenever I share wid a young'un, I pay back a goodness that befell me," said Lester. "A magnif'cence like dis reminds us that dere is a God up in heaven," he said.

As he unlocked the doors, the trills and arpeggios of Bach's *Toccata and Fugue* met and surrounded us, punctuated with the chirps of a single sparrow. The arched ribs of the chapel traveled upward, five to seven times higher than the library. Music from the organ trellised the Hillsborough-stone walls, welcoming us to the nave. The sparrow flitted, banked, and dove

JAMES GHOLSON, JR.

about, a visual commentary on the music emanating from the tower. Lester placed a forefinger vertically on his lips and waved me forward. I followed him, finger tipping the crusty texture of several stone bricks, toward the steps of the tower. It was a singular treat to witness the chapel in its colorful, realistic glory in comparison to the black-and-white sketches I'd seen and copied. I climbed the tower stairs—and took several pictures of the stairwell from the top and bottom. In spite of slight vertigo, my spirit sailed past trembling to exhilaration, as if I were seeing through the eye of Abele, from carillon to crypt. I admit that a split-second of trepidation—from my sloping slide above the Capitol Dome—*came back!* Lester said a brief prayer . . . "Our Father . . ."

XV

They'd met—one as caterer, the other as socialite and personal adviser—in the Argentine Embassy, a handsome, well-crafted building which stood at 1600 New Hampshire Avenue, near Embassy Row, in Washington, D.C. Now they sat in the office of the elder woman, sliced by sunlight from Venetian blinds, with a vocal parakeet in the shadows.

The bird was an especially precocious participant and chirped, "Party time," with reckless fervor.

The woman, known in D.C. circles as a savant, was especially charming; some would add motherly, to the young girl who was impressed by the woman's continental manner, the ease with which she slipped in and out of several languages—French, Spanish, English—in genteel conversation with party attendees. The girl was there as a caterer from the Uptown Grill and tightly masked her spellbound gawks, feet glued to the floor, at the spectacular exhibit of wealth—jewels, diamond rings, necklaces and tie pins, embroidered silk blouses and shirts—that sparkled and glistened around her. The elder woman, intrigued by the raw beauty of the young caterer, sensed some psychic asymmetry challenging the youth. Speaking to the girl—first in Greek, then French, and finally in English—the woman said, "Do come see me so we can chat," and slipped Samantha her business card.

The girl was transfixed by the attention she'd received and smiled. "Okay." The woman brushed back an errant lock of Samantha's hair and promptly engaged conversation, in another tongue, with partygoers.

Now the woman sat on a large yellow fit ball, a turban on her head, wearing a tan leisure suit. "Party time, party," sang the parakeet, and the girl laughed and said, "That's so cute; it's almost as if he were right at the grill where I work."

On the wall of the office was a large picture of Harriet Tubman. "Oh yes, he's a big partygoer and loves to hear the music and watch the ladies. Is your beau anything like that?"

Samantha reflected for a moment and bathed in the attention and interest the woman showed in her. At this moment she felt herself to be the center of the universe. It was a moment uniquely unlike any she'd experienced. "Oh no, kinda quiet and studious;

but he does love people," adding quietly, "a few of the girls in my sorority don't like him."

That comment received a mental check mark by the turbaned woman. She said, "And I'm sure that you love him—would that be accurate?"

"I'm just not sure anymore. We've been together for more than a year. I thought I had found just the perfect guy for myself. I lived in the dorm when I first came to campus. We started hanging out afterward to study and eat—it was months before we slept together."

"And do you like the same kind of music?" said the woman, her face and trunk relaxed as she slid back and forth, straddling the exercise ball, adding, "I know my tastes in music developed when I attended college. We heard Cuban popular music and a good bit of the Motown sound where I grew up, but then I also attended the symphony, and I grew to see new relationships, even between classical and popular music."

"Oh, he likes just about any kind of music; he played cello in high school and for a year at Harrison, but his studies started to take over in his sophomore and junior years," said Samantha as her eyelids drooped just a bit. "He has invited me to hear the orchestra downtown, but I never seem to quite make it."

"I see," said the woman, rising from the exercise ball now and striding slowly to the chair behind her desk.

"Party time," chirped the parakeet, cooing in the shadows.

The woman took her seat and smiled. "And do you like the cello? Could you stand to hear the cello early in the morning, perhaps?"

"Well, I guess it would be okay. I mean, I kinda listened to it at first—you know—like it was a novelty," and the girl giggled belatedly. "I thought he would sing along with it, sing me a serenade-like song."

"Pieces of eight, party hearty," said the parakeet. The woman gave the bird a cracker.

"And what is your field? What are you studying—hospitality?"

"I'm not quite sure about that either," said Samantha, slipping deeper into her chair, looking more relaxed. "My mom thinks that hospitality is a fun field. She likes the cello and once saw a musician playing the violin in a hospital."

"I always loved the cello—its deep rich sounds—I tried to play it once, but my arm caught a cramp, and I took that as a negative sign." They both laughed.

"Pieces of eight, party, party!"

"Let me make you some tea." Samantha nodded

her approval. "Does chamomile meet with your approval?" Samantha nodded in affirmation.

"You know, I sang in my church choir for a while when I was growing up, and then for a while in the gospel choir too for two years. I just lost interest in it."

"Now you work as a caterer, and that can bring in some extra money. You say you are from Morgantown, West Virginia. I checked, and there are not a lot of black folk there. Uptown Bar and Grill does a good bit of work for the Argentine Embassy. I was happy to be able to meet you there. How did you get 'hooked up,'—as you Americans say—with them?"

"Well, several—"

"Here's your tea ... forgive my interruption ..."

Samantha continued. "Several of us from my sorority go there for meetings and jus' to get away from campus to talk. They let us have a meeting or two there also, from time to time. Trevor, he's the son of the owner, goes to Harrison, and he's from right here in the city, so he knows his way around. But he's in the same fraternity with Caleb, my boyfriend. Their fraternity comes around to serenade us—sing to us—with songs about girl and boys things, let us know that we are cherished and appreciated. It's a lot of fun, and I enjoy the sorority life."

"And you," said the turbaned woman, "you feel appreciated and cherished. I mean you are young and quite beautiful. Surely you feel adored. And you tell me that you are now wearing this miner's hard hat from West Virginia so that you feel safe on campus. Hilarious!" They both had a hearty laugh and took copious swigs of tea.

"This tea is great. I'll have to keep some around. Anyway—yes, my dad sent it to me. He had it outfitted with a videotape camera—a really small one—that records me moving about campus. He calls it my 'security hard hat.' Me coming from mining country, nobody seems to mind if I bop around on campus with it; they jus' think that it's kinda country, backwoods behavior."

"I see, and this Trevor fellow, how do your sorority girlfriends relate—how do they like him?"

"Oh, fine, like a naughty brother or something. Occasionally, he gets a little fresh."

"Fresh ... What does that mean?"

"Play and things, like he wants me to go out with him, but I straighten him out real fast."

"And these friends that like him, are they the same ones that don't like Caleb?"

"They think him to be too independent; too square around the edges, jus' not in tune with Greek agendas."

"Party pieces of eight, party hearty," chimed the parakeet.

"You mean the hard partying type?"

"Yes, that sounds about right. Right now, I'm in the Special Education program. I want to be a teacher and help unfortunate students learn."

"So maybe it's time to have the sorority girls get to know Caleb a little better. Or, have the girls over to the frat house, so that they can interact. You say your sorority was serenaded by Caleb and his group? How did that go?"

The girl stiffened visibly, and it took some time for her to speak. She drained the rest of tea in her cup as the parakeet spoke. "Party time, hearty party . . . party time!"

"And," asked the older woman, "do you think those kinds of conversations—this mutual sharing—is better afforded around drinks or cigarettes or weed?" The woman brushed the upper half of her silken leisure suit which revealed ample breasts flowering her torso. The fabric and color added contrast to her slightly reddish complexion, allowing her neck and head to flower in the style of Georgia O'Keefe.

"The girls I know best now are those who live at the sorority house. Sometimes the conversations get a little raunchy, and they discuss how they manipulate the guys they date, what they want from them,

JAMES GHOLSON, JR.

and how they negotiate sex with them—what and how they reward guys to get what they want. Some of the fellas are athletes and headed toward making gobs of money. They say that the intellectual types—those types who think about fairness and equity—are a pain in the butt. Basically, what they, as women, like, and how they like it. Those conversations were totally new to me. Anyway, one of the girls said she saw Caleb walking across campus with a new girlfriend, said I should throw my keys to his apartment at him when we had the next serenade.

"May I smoke?" said Samantha.

"We'll smoke together," said the woman known as Dr. Ramona.

In the fog of cigarette smoke, Samantha continued. "They call me Sam in the sorority house. Some of the bull sessions are amazing and horrendously funny. My closest friend, Candy, has a hookup who adores her stinky drawers. I mean, this guy sends her flowers and quality clothing she wears around school. She adores wearing it—modeling this stuff—around the sorority house and caricatures talking with this guy. She made a clay model of his D . . . uh, private parts, as if it were a ventriloquist's dummy, and puts on little plays, or recites Shakespearean sonnets as if she were having sex discussions:

SKULLY

Roses have thorns, and silver fountains mud;
Clouds and eclipses stain
both moon and sun,
And loathsome canker lives in sweetest bud.

"She is an amazing actress. That dildo head, shaped like a penis, is practically an exact replica of her boyfriend's face. Anyway, to answer your question, Trevor is like my bulldog, my protector. Before college, he attended boarding school. He devised a way we would get that key-throwing stuff done and," she reached in her purse to pull out the "Tumbleweed" photo. "This is what happened." She shared the photo with the older woman.

"Oh my," said the older woman, exhaling a long stream of cigarette smoke in the direction of the Venetian blinds, then placing her fingers across her lips. "So, have you and Caleb spoken since this happened? If not, then perhaps I can be of service to you. But I will have to request that you both come, tout ensemble, together. Oh, my child, I do hope that you—*we*—can work on this together. I am sure you have many admirers, now and in the future. It is healthy to understand the nature of magnetism between men and women, if only to sidestep unnecessary heartbreak. You say this Trevor graduated from boarding school? Then I would suppose that

JAMES GHOLSON, JR.

his manners and social carriage are impeccable, and he is under your spell, so to speak."

Samantha managed a stiff chuckle. "Oh yes. His uncle owns the restaurant—the Uptown Grill—where I work."

Neither woman realized that the building in which they first met was purchased on February 20, 1913, by the Argentine government from Mrs. Henrietta Huff, who decided to sell the house after her husband's death in 1912. The designer of the building was Philadelphia native Julian Abele (1881–1950). It certainly would have given Samantha and Caleb a lot to see and talk about had they known. Mr. Huff commissioned architect Horace Trumbauer to design the house in 1906.

XVI

"Do you think I could have forgotten your voice so easily?" That was the sentence delivered by Caleb Fentress when Bach's *Toccata and Fugue* sang on his phone as he jaywalked into traffic on Georgia Avenue against the light. A hot shower had started his day. For breakfast: granola and yogurt, orange juice, and coffee. For dress: a green-based madras shirt with splashes of red, black slacks, black socks over the calf, slouch hat, and no dark glasses. For organization: all sketches done in Durham, snapshots taken in Durham; and for leisure: swimming trunks, goggles, soap, and a towel. Birds trilled and chirped as he made his way to campus. He hummed the tune of "To Canaan" as he walked, not remembering the words, unsure of where the tune came from. Buses roared up and down the street leaving small clouds of diesel smoke behind. All his business accoutrements were housed in his backpack.

Here and there, Knock Out Roses budded but were yet to bloom. He moved with purpose, with a quick step and a list in one hand. He had yet to hear the word "Tumbleweed" and took that as a good sign. Passing one coffee house, he inhaled deeply and heard strains of "Drumma Boy's Shawty" come from somewhere inside as he weaved his way down the sidewalk. Bach's *Toccata and Fugue* sang on his phone. He pulled the phone from his pocket and answered it brusquely with, "Caleb."

"Hi, Caleb," said Samantha, "remember me?"

"Do you think I could have forgotten your voice so easily?" he answered, feeling his nature rise in an urgency that only swimming—or a woman—could cure.

"Am I calling at a bad time?" she asked. He'd narrowly missed becoming a nonliving, breathless shadow on pavement as a car swerved to miss him.

After crossing the street, he said, "Nope, all good; headed to campus to run some errands and do classes. I know who you are. Whassup?"

"We haven't spoken in a while; I wanted—needed—to talk with you, see how you are and ask you something. I heard that you were awarded a nice internship for the summer. Congratulations!"

"Yep. Been very lucky, and Dean Davenport has been like a guardian angel along the way. I finally have been able to understand the way he pushes and guides. You good?"

"For the most part," said Samantha. "The girls at the house keep me in stitches, and classes are going okay."

Caleb waved to a few of his buddies—leaving the phone to his ear—and turned up the volume, slowed his gait.

"Are you busy all day?" asked Samantha. Her voice had a slight tremor in it, like it did when they fondled. His physical urge became stronger, and he noticed himself gripping the list tighter. He saw the geometry of her lips in his mind's eye, the taunt nipples of her breasts. *Yeah, bud, it has been awhile.*

He refocused. "Well, I have some major errands to run, but I have an idea. I think it's probably better to talk away from—off campus—since I have a lot to say and am sure you do. That way, we could get away from the eyes and ears on campus, get to the bottom of things." The word *bottom* seemed to stick in his throat; his imagination successfully eluded the tight grip of his hand, and he saw her wonderful legs, long and golden to the waist, glow in the blazing sunshine of the morning.

"I know you are probably right. I won't ask my question right now, but would enjoy seeing you and having a chance to talk. What I did was very adolescent, and—"

"We'll talk about it. Like I said, I have been tremendously lucky and learned a lot lately. I may have been a little overly sensitive. But, as you can imagine, I was very, very pissed." I could smell Samantha, her hair, taste her skin, feel the touch of her hands right there on the sidewalk of Georgia Avenue. "Where will you be?" said Caleb, hoping that he would pick her up away from the sorority house.

"I have a class with two of my sisters; we are supposed to study a bit at the sorority house."

"Okay," he said, "Let's say around five or so. It will be good to see you."

"Bye, Caleb," said Samantha.

Caleb had written down some basic words in Greek. He also saved the same ones on his cell phone. Words like "kalimera" for hello and for good-bye "kalispera." That was taxing enough for the few minutes he needed to walk from his spot to the Anatomy Department. *My knowledge of Greek is limited to the Greek alphabet, thanks to the fraternity pledge period. Work on the language app on your phone. Fortunately, there are a ton of Greek restaurants in D.C. Buy a map of Greece.*

Lara was in class when he stopped by the Anatomy Department, and Dean Davenport was in meetings.

He left notes for both. For Lara, he wrote, "*Can you send me a few of the Tumbleweed photos? How's Skully?*" And for the dean, he wrote, "*Got some great shots and good sketches down at Duke. Thanks for the suggestion on Abele. Am trying to make the images dream!*"

Samantha, along with her sorority friends, headed for the sorority house after discussions about the test bank they wanted to establish in mathematics and cybersecurity classes. They met at the Upton Bar and Grill. Trevor drove them to the sorority house around three thirty. Samantha had worn her canary-yellow miner's hard hat most of the day. *This thing is hot and makes my hair and scalp feel musty*, she thought to herself. Candy had skipped eating at lunch; she wanted to drop fifty pounds.

"Need to lose more'n fifty if you ask me," said Trevor as he let them out of the car in front of the sorority house. Candy overheard the wisecrack and scowled at him.

Julie said, "That's not nice, Trevor."

Samantha laughed and said, "Naughty boy—send me the specifics on that Sunday night gig. I'm busy tonight." Once she had arrived at the house, she took a long shower and joked with Candy and Julie, who lived in upstairs rooms at the sorority house.

Julie worked in several of the downtown department stores as a model, often receiving free or discounted apparel as payment. She kept a large cache of clothes on a movable clothes rack. She and Samantha wore similar sizes. The girls bounded up steps, anxious to chat about Lara's date with Caleb, anxious to see if they could plunder Julie's wardrobe for a fetching outfit designed to tease.

Once inside, Julie said, "Well, if you're digging Trevor, then you should have a real serious conversation with Caleb. Ain't no telling how he perceives you now, you throwing his keys at him and all." In half an hour, they had torched half of the wardrobe and were still short of the look they wanted.

"Black is definitely out; much too formal," said Julie.

"I like green, dark green," said Candy, to which Samantha replied, "Makes me look fat," and they all cracked up. They had finalized Samantha's look by four forty-five.

"Fluff," said Julie. A yellow A-line dress, wide black belt, a white sweater with the sleeves tied around the neck, and white tennis shoes.

By this time, Candy had fetched her brown dildo-puppet and was conversing with it, saying "No no no—hands off. What you see is what you do *not* get! Down, boy." The doorbell downstairs rang and Candy flew down the stairs to answer it. "'Tumbleweed' is here, y'all!"

"Hey, Candy, what's up?"

"Nada, Caleb," said Candy, "Congrats on your externship. She'll be right down," and bounced back up the stairs.

Just as Caleb sat down, Bach's *Toccata and Fugue* sang from his phone. *Lara!* The tune seemed to play endlessly as he fumbled to lower its volume. *Answer or send to voice mail?* He decided on the latter and brought up his calendar to etch in a reminder.

"Hi, Caleb." said Samantha. "You remembered my voice . . . remember me?"

"No doubt! Ready?" asked Caleb. "You look nice."

"Thank you," she said, and they headed to the waiting cab. "Was just thinking that your steps are even higher than the ones at the frat house; glad I wasn't sitting on these!" Samantha poked him in the ribs.

"Where're you headed?" said the cabbie.

"Union Station," said Caleb.

"Dean Davenport gave me a sketch done by Julian Abele, an architect from Philly," said Caleb as the cab took them down Massachusetts Avenue. "Abele studied in Europe during the Impressionistic Period—Debussy, Lautrec, Monet—and his purpose was to absorb as much as possible of Western artistic technique and ethos. He designed Duke University's Western Campus. I was awestruck seeing his spectacular sketches and designs online. I wanted to see them live for myself—and plumb what he learned and how he applied it to his creations. It was a terrific experience."

"Are you still angry with me? You must be, 'cause you often share that kinda stuff with me."

"I was disgusted with what you did, Samantha—beyond angry. We've been together a year and a half, nightly. You *know* me; I never ever contrived to embarrass you in public. And you have not offered me a reason why you did this—which adds to my confusion," said Caleb.

"I am truly sorry it worked out that way. It was supposed to be a prank. I just found a personal advisor," said Samantha. "She asked if I would bring my beau—my lover, who is you—to my next session."

Union Station stood in luminous grandeur, never more beautiful than now: creamy, busy, phosphorescent, with lights on as dusk turned to dark. Pigeons strutted about the pavement, flocking here and there, searching for peanuts and popcorn kernels. Samantha looked like a Greek goddess as she strolled to the table; she never took her eyes off Caleb. Caleb stood before her, just for a second as the sunset approached its end, looking squarely into her eyes.

"Since we met, there has been no one but you. I have said I love you more to you than even my parents." They sat down at a table in the outer foyer. "Based on some slanderous gossip, some bizarre chatter by some decrepit asshole—based on their *words*, you chose a love ceremony dedicated to *your* sorority and *our* sweetheart, to humiliate me in front of my campus brotherhood. It was not your fault that it ended up in the papers, on the front page. But I was so embarrassed. First, you must—you should—explain it to me—"

The waiter before them said, "May I get you something?"

"Yes," said Caleb, "two waters with ice. We'll be ready when you get back." He looked at Samantha, studied her face. Shadows of travelers blended and washed in the mix of indoor and fading outdoor light.

"What are you having?" said Samantha.

"Just a tuna salad; nothing heavy; and a beer."

"I think I'll have the crab cakes and rice with a side salad," she said.

"So you want me to go with you to see your advisor?" said Caleb.

"Exactly, Caleb. She is a relationship counselor and wants to work with us together."

"This is a challenging time for me, Sam. I have my hands full getting ready for the summer. Let me think about it and call you. That is the best I can do," he said. "We have been together, you and I, almost every night since we met. You took someone else's word over what you experience in the flesh every day and *acted* on it. How on earth can that be?"

The waiter returned, and they ordered. "One tuna salad, a crab special, and two beers—Michelobs."

Desire tantalized their appetites, teased their silences, and strutted up and down the station's tunnels.

"And your mom, she is good?" Samantha's words struck him as stiff.

"Oh yeah, she's fine—a little worried about Dad's friend Jesse. He's been sick on and off. He gave me a gift that I had examined at the Anatomy Deportment. Sam, just for the record, I would like to know who corralled you into doing what you did."

"It was a silly thing to do, and I am sorry, Caleb, very sorry. My sorors—some of them—are a crazy bunch and often say things, hurtful things, to people. You shouldn't take it personally."

"Like *Tumbleweed?* No problem. I do take *you* personally, and that makes it hurt—humbles our garden, tumbles our love."

"So your answer is no?"

"I'll let you know."

It was almost eleven when they quit Union Station. The pigeons had evaporated into the humid darkness haunting the Capitol Dome. Reflections of that Dome oscillated with images of Skully on the cab windows in the visions of Caleb; for Samantha, it grew scumbled in the tones of Caleb's reddish-walnut skin. The cab took them uptown.

XVII

The magical aura of Samantha shone even during the silences of our dinner together. It was obvious that a strong physical attraction existed between us; my concern revolved around our mental affinities. I suspected that Candy had engineered the "Tumbleweed" affair; perhaps Trevor was involved. Coupled with his predilection for boarding school pranks, "Tumbleweed" had his fingerprint. Sprayed and skewered with water as I attempted to catch my keys, I had skidded down the steps of the frat house onto pavement and been humiliated by front-page photos in the newspapers—wet and embarrassed; but there was a gift in it!

My sweaty dream suggested a bizarre answer. Skully was the Capital Dome; my ski down the waves of water into the Potomac was the image I needed to rivet my mind to creativity—the red tongue of the green Chinese dragon moving down

SKULLY

New Hampshire Avenue, the scene of sorority pledges, engineers of that dragon, brought me face-to-face with a creative side of the issue. How would I milk the magical message of my dream, ride this parable of Skully to fuel my destiny, and mine the gifts of Julian Abele? How would I engage the image, possess it to my favor, tease it in retrograde, in mirrors echoed and inverted, and capture it—in piece or whole—in metals, glasses, transparencies, and blueprints, digitized on paper and trapped for my own conceptions. I saw Skully as an ice cube—saw it dive to the bottom of my glass of water—pushed by my straw—tumble, spin, and bobble back to the top, laughing as it bubbled and refloated; *resilience.* Sam gave me this image—tumbling down stairs, swept from the Capital Dome, thrown into the Potomac, and witnessed by thousands of waves to be likewise seen and reflected by them. Could I possibly channel myself as a many-eyed dragonfly to know the wonder and creativity in those images?

The slope of my fall was almost forty-five degrees. It was a slope of images in motion—Skully as dome; Abele as key; a hose as torrential water; stairsteps as altitudes—and a fiery dragon in the Potomac as a hopeless abyss. Luckily, I had broken nothing; no teeth, arms, legs, or my noggin. There was a lesson in that, and maybe even more lessons in the shadows of the event. Occasionally during dinner, I blew bubbles under those ice cubes with my straw; the turbulence caused renewed spinning and bobbles. Even pushed with the straw, they rose to the water's top. I observed their rise, referenced by small waves around them: lightness and shadows. But the biggest question of all—given the developments undertaken by Lara—was ... *Where on earth did Skully rise from?*

Time was not on my side when I boarded my flight for Greece. I had only superficially learned basic Greek greetings and requests, even with visiting local Greek restaurants, and my reading knowledge was toilet worthy. My Internet surfing had given me a sense of the Acropolis Museum and an overview of the Athens neighborhood. As we approached our landing, I could see the ancient ruins of the Byzantine period, the Acropolis itself, and the museum from the sky.

Lara had promised to keep me updated on Skully, Mom had promised to update me on Jesse, Dean Davenport had encouraged me—based on my Durham sketches—to continue these efforts in Athens, and Samantha had sent a rather brusque note thanking me for dinner. To say that I was brimming with confidence would be an overstatement. Seeing the Acropolis live from the plane was a wonderful treat. I reflected on Davenport's words: *"Plant your first few steps on the ground with respect of the democratic history of the place."* In my mind, I saw my own frat, high-stepping to the strains of "To Canaan," swinging and swaying down New Hampshire Avenue, determined to crash into the "Promised Land," by hook or crook. *"We can add those to your portfolio; some of these you made in Durham are very good,"* said Davenport.

Poor Lara was concerned that a visit by the coroner's office and detectives to Jesse at the church had so upset him that he had fallen ill; she blamed herself. Unfortunately, he had not shared new information on Skully's origin. All he said to the authorities was, "That skull be older than dirt." That was later to be confirmed, but who knows how old dirt is?

My externship responsibilities included odd jobs around Acropolis Museum offices, explaining the American architectural curriculum to Greek students, demonstrating teaching techniques with which I was familiar, and running errands for administrators in the main office. I had freedom to take in seminars and classes that did not conflict with the needs of my superiors. I loved this arrangement and followed many of the precepts of time and skill tactics that were developed in Durham. I decided to practice by taking random pictures of the Parthenon and making sketches of each. I warmed up making copies of the stairwell of Duke's Chapel Tower; it was my left- and right-handed warm-up exercise. I called it "Abele's Eye."

The Acropolis Museum stood as a result of a competition in architectural design. Its beauty is primal and exhibits lightness—glass floors—and classical tripartite structural eloquence. A multiplicity of structural pillars and "see-through" floors give the building transparency. Three layers of slightly angled horizontal layers allow the museum to pay homage to its neighbors, especially the Parthenon, the Old Temple of Athena, and the Theater of Dionysus. All this was seen with singular clarity from the holding pattern of my plane. I felt the plane's wings as my own, beating in the breeze, its engines roar as my heart, its posture arc in the sky as if I piloted gyroscopic, and joy as we nestled safely grounded: *dragonfly mode*.

Below transparent glass floors carefully groomed in situ, the ruins of an ancient Athens neighborhood, gently and painstakingly revealed as an archaeological dig: mosaic floors, cistern, dining area, they all sparkled. Numerous artifacts, revealed in varying degrees of modesty, objects recovered from temples and sanctuaries decorated this grand smorgasbord of visual delight. Immediately, Jesse's small archaeological dig came to mind. I wondered at what point Skully's imagination—his sense of creativity and wonder—had ceased. *Has he seen and accomplished his mission? Hovered dragonfly mode? A dragonfly has twenty-eight thousand telescoping lenses enabling three hundred and sixty degrees of vision; Skully's vision equaled a big fat zero.* My Nikon clicked overtime under my fingers; my sketched copying persisted, but never caught up, and my legs ached from the walking I did in my first few days. After about two weeks, Khromis, a staff worker in the administrative office, invited me to speak about American architecture at a summer session of an architectural design group.

"What are you learning about how we do things in Greece?" he asked.

"Well, of course, I love working at the museum," I said. "Being in the midst of such historic surroundings and seeing how Greeks value their techniques of construction as developed and refined over many years—this is something that I have become much more aware of. I haven't gotten to visit many construction firms and watched them coordinate with design people and construction engineers to see exactly how that works."

We bantered a bit about principles of democratic

JAMES GHOLSON, JR.

participation, Socratic discussion, and philosophies of architectural design. I was pleasantly surprised to know that a few participants knew of Abele and the genius of his work on the Duke campus. I had many of the photos and a few sketches I'd made at Duke and talked through them with the group. Additionally, I spoke about Abele's background and younger years; the Colored Institute in Philadelphia, which later became Cheyney State, the Union League (140 S. Broad Street, also in Philadelphia) founded to support the military politics of Abraham Lincoln. "I didn't know that Jim Crow politics were actually legal repressive laws," said one listener.

There was considerable discussion about the "exedra" concept and his consummate design of the Conklin Gate at Haverford College. "Is that how democracy works in the USA—treating a man of such talent with lifelong repression?" I had raised the same questions personally; on foreign soil I was embarrassed by it. I said, "Well, he understood the repression that existed during his time, so he worked in the *shadows*."

In the third week of my fellowship, Mom called to say that Jesse had died. The revelation shook me up a good bit, especially since he had been kind enough to be my benefactor and because he was the sole connector to the riddle of Skully. I was sure that

I could wrangle some bit of information from him that would connect the dots and lead me to the origin of Skully, the truth of Skully's existence. Now, that was gone, primarily because I had just flat run out of time. Mom said she was going to the funeral. I called Khromis on my phone.

"Khromis, you real busy?"

"Not really," he said, turning down some folk music in the background.

"Let's go get something to eat and a drink or two. I'll stop by your apartment."

"Okay," he said with delight.

Like many major cities, Athens had significant problems with the homeless. Khromis and I walked from his place to a nearby restaurant. On the way, we talked. "How'd you like that session, Caleb? I thought the questions were pretty good, kinda tough for you at points." Khromis had been to the States and had at least visually seen American racism in action.

"Anytime you have unfairness there is bitterness, Khromis. Look around at your homeless folks here in Athens," I said. "We've tried democracy all over the earth, and still in its cradle or even in my country, people live on the streets," I said.

A woman begged Khromis for something, and he just waved her off. "She wants a blanket. So, Caleb, are you homesick yet?"

"I think I am getting homesick. A close family friend died yesterday. My mom just called me about it. He gave me a gift before I left to come here. It has been a most perplexing gift, and I should have been there to honor a request he made to me about it. This gyro is really good."

"Sometimes it is impossible to get everything done. Then you start to feel guilty, even downtrodden about it, and get even less done." We laughed and toasted to getting less done. "So what happens when you get back to the States?"

"Well, this is my last year coming up, so I'm job hunting officially when I get back." We ordered small salads to go with the gyros. "I've had a great time in Athens, and playtime is over, so it's time to get down to business, polish my portfolio, and get to work," I said.

As we walked back from the restaurant, I spotted these beautiful golden legs and buttocks—splendidly exposed, since the back of her black dress lay completely exposed and open. That reminded me of Samantha. Her casual stride, both bold and languid, spoke directly to my loins, mesmerized my eyes, and fraught me with vivid reminders of our lovemaking. Khromis noticed my stare and commented comically, "My friend, I see you are entranced with this female in front of us. Even though she is a prostitute, I will call her for you." When addressed, she turned, revealing an unusually pale, toothless face housed inside a coal-black hood, and the sagging breasts of a nag. Words froze in my mouth, and my capacity to respond fell—facedown—into the street.

"Prostitution is legal in Greece," said Khromis.

"Her face looks like that of a skull," I said to Khromis, who chuckled.

"A story for you, my friend." Early on, Khromis had taken me to see *Elektra*, a play by Sophocles with a Greek chorus about power and revenge; now he spoke of Thucydides, who called Kerameikos the most beautiful suburb of ancient Athens. "Some years ago, archaeologists were involved in the dig for the Kerameikos subway station. Excavators there discovered the skeletons of men, women, and children, all thrown pell-mell into a common pit, without ceremony or the least mark of respect. We struggle here, as do all countries, with enabling the best in mankind."

XVIII

I was truly wiped out on my return trip to American soil. I had purchased trinkets for Lara and Samantha, Dean Davenport and Mom. My preflight dreams were populated with skulls, dragonflies, and all manner of lime-green dragons. My best sketches were in my backpack, and my photos stored in digital clouds online. My Greek colleagues sent us off with a party for all the fellowship externs, and I nursed a wee bit of a hangover before the flight. Abele had traveled all over Europe—France, Germany, Italy—to nourish his talent and made a remarkable effort to tower over circumstances and validate his genius through concrete works of art. Compared to his, my efforts seemed tawdry.

Also, I received text messages from both Samantha and Lara. Lara assured me that Skully was clear of all questions, saying, "Our distinguished skull rests comfortably in its glass cage, respectful in

SKULLY

its silent glare, humbly listening for refrains of 'To Canaan.' Out of curiosity, artist friends of mine and one from the police dept. had drawn sketches of what they think Skully looked like as a young person. Very handsome! Yr friend, Lara." Samantha's text read, "Dear Tumbleweed: I know you were pressed for time when you left; you haven't said if you will visit my adviser with me when you get back. I know that on some level you still care about me, or that is what I prefer to think. Summer classes are all good and D.C. weather is sticky, muggy, hot, and humid, but then, what difference can you expect in a swamp? Luv, Sam."

My worldview had expanded considerably, and I felt my friendship with Khromis would last a lifetime, though who could know that at the time? His perspectives brought a realm of color and wise intuition to personal observation that I valued. Personally, I felt as though I had an expanded worldview. I'd gained a new conception of Greek culture—food, music, theater, and art—while at the same time growing as a raconteur and communicator.

My left-handed sketches had finally improved (after dogged persistence), and my watercolors ceased showing a prevailing muddiness. Aboard the jumbo jet, I slept soundly; the plane was packed to the gills. I was happy to be on the way home. In some ways, I tried to reconcile the history of democracy with the realities of slavery, written, oral, and psychic. Overwhelmed in my effort to come to grips with that, I targeted education and economics as issues requiring national attention. I wondered anew why institutions of color had abandoned economic boycotts as a means of tackling poor accomplishments in diversity and black employment. In my thoughts, I lambasted institutions of higher education for their absence from the education fray in inner cities, especially in the era of the Internet. To my mind, black institutions—the NAACP and Urban League—seemed gawky and graceless as strategists on the spectral sway of Jesse's gold watch, neglecting strategies of both black cultural nationalism and cultural integration. I dozed on and off, thinking of the great black leaders of the sixties. *Had blacks been compromised, seduced by materialism?*

In broad swaths of every state, racial hostility persisted, solely based on skin color, with many boards of directors content to actively eschew developing new avenues of exposure, education, or reconciliation with fresh platforms for the "great artistic antiquities of the West" to persons of color. The very things that would encourage American pride, develop commitment to democratic ideals, and a personal stake in losing exquisite treatment—learning the tools of the West—were

SKULLY

the very instruments *withheld* in exploitation, foreign and domestic, of cultural cleavages. With classical arts sidelined, popular art, music, and theater ruled the roost. The intricate emotional and intellectual meticulousness of the classical arts waxed passé.

Was the volcanic anger and hatred of a young Malcolm X justified? How justified is the perennial peace and love espoused by Martin King? Or the self-sufficiency of Booker T.? Where is the awesome *effort* of Harriet Tubman in championing full humanity of black persons to access, digital and otherwise, in contemporary American culture—old pistol-packing Harriet, totally focused on the North Star?

"Musta escorted one-thousand slaves to freedom; *coulda saved even more, if they knew they were slaves.*" I lapsed in and out of consciousness, my thoughts gobbling up territory like a jet engine, the crisp dialogue of *Elektra* in one ear, the stark whirl of Skully as Yorick in Shakespeare's *Hamlet*.

"Alas, poor [Skully] Yorick! I knew him, Horatio: a fellow of infinite jest, of most excellent fancy: he hath borne me on his back a thousand times; and now, how abhorred in my imagination it is!"

Who could know what Jesse's skull had seen? But Jesse had put me on his back; I felt taunted by his humble request, "Well, if there is no other way, bury him alongside me."

We landed at Dulles International, in the land of the free and the home of the brave. I did not wait to exhale or plant both feet on American soil.

"Caleb! You look so good," said Mom when we met at baggage claim. "I am so happy to see you," and she hugged me and gave me a kiss on the cheek. I had not expected anyone and surprised myself by my elation. "Here, I brought along a program from Jessie's funeral; they're having a memorial service for him in Memphis." Immediately, my thoughts turned to Memphis. *Gotta get down there!* I said, "Oh! Say, Mom, how did you get out here—you drive?"

"Oh, she didn't tell you?" said Mom. "I can't remember her name."

We had to wait fifteen to twenty minutes for the baggage carousel to start rolling, and Mom—bless her seventy-year-old soul—reflected on Jesse and said, "I'm so sorry about Jesse . . ."

She—whoever *she* was—sneaked up behind me and covered my eyes on her return. She said, "Do you remember my name?"

I said, "Of course I remember your name." Feeling the warmth of her full body close behind me and not wanting to play the fool, I said, "Samantha, it's good to feel you."

"Nope, guess again, brown brother."

My heart sank, and I felt more embarrassed. I

guessed again, "Lara?" which drew this response, "Finally," she said, waving her finger from side to side.

We hugged vigorously as her neck arched away from me, her arms locked around my waist. I wondered if she had felt my sex extend itself toward her, stiff with desire, and hoped she hadn't noticed me blush. I said, "Fancy meeting you here," and cast a curious eye toward Mom.

XIV

I hadn't got in to see the dean right away. Once Lara and I took Mom home, we hung out for a while (Mom loaned me her car) talking, and I shared Greek photos and drawings with her. I also apologized for the rock-solid hard-on which she must have felt. She was drinking a tall glass of iced-tea. Her guffaw lifted a geyser of tea-spray across the room. Stunned patrons sitting nearby ducked and scrambled for cover—laughter and disgust mixed fifty-fifty.

She said, "Oh, Caleb, I took it as a compliment!" Intuition suggested to me that I share with Lara my intent to visit Samantha's shrink and to deal with things as professionally as possible. Lara agreed.

"Boy, you have done me so very, very proud," said Dean Davenport, "and your grades from last semester exhaled fire and sprouted wings . . . kept 'em right here in my office so you wouldn't be worried about 'em. They loved you in Greece; I spoke to the embassy just yesterday." Davenport exploded with praise for my externship (he called it a fellowship) contributions and added, "Glory be!" I had forgotten all about my grades, but figured I was doing well.

"I tightened up my reading concentration and used index cards to solidify my knowledge base," I said. "I have a family friend—had a family friend—Jesse, who counseled me to think in three dimensions."

"Excellent advice, son, excellent. I remember now, something about thinking in the past, present, and future all at once! Now I have this prospect for you, son ... may have mentioned it ... been thinking you should enter this competition. Remember when we spoke about it—let's see, I think it was around the time you mentioned him before—can't fully recall, but I read your friend Jesse's obituary in the paper and noticed that he was from Memphis. Strange, I grew up not too far from there in Brownsville, Tennessee. You ever been to Memphis? Interesting town, damn interesting," he said clipping a cigar. "Whenever I think of Memphis—Martin King, Ida Wells, Richard Wright, Sterling Brown—those names, a stellar array of freedom fighters, come to mind. I think mainly of the Fort Pillow Massacre, which this competition is about. Tennessee is holding a competition to honor the soldiers who died in that battle; amazing!"

JAMES GHOLSON, JR.

"Fort Pillow," I said dumbfounded. "I never heard of the place."

"Well, you kids that grew up in the East got Civil War history that dealt mainly with the eastern theater and not quite as much about developments in the western theater. But you both got—have you got time for this?" he said looking at me quizzically as I nodded assent, "—got that *insane* bullshit that blacks were happy darkies back on the plantation, nothing 'bout what *really* happened, the escapes, the spying, whipping posts, and the plots and planning, the black fellas joining the Union Army. Hell, one half-assed Southern scholar compared old Nathan Forrest—he was the winner of that battle—compared him to Abe Lincoln; called him a damn genius! Anyway, got off on a tangent. Blacks and most historians call Fort Pillow a massacre. Dixiecrats and unvarnished Rebels call it an *incident* or *affair*. Fools! You know black men got the gun before they got an education, later had to fight jus' to go to school. Hate to think that is the reason we have such carnage in the streets today—guns before education—dudes can't read or cipher. Anyway, this is a design competition that is requesting entries that honor the fallen, both black artillerists and cavalry, at Fort Pillow. There are a lot of hard feelings about Fort Pillow down in West Tennessee, with a statue glorifying Nathan Bedford right in the middle of Memphis. Now, this competition, sponsored by the Park Service, is looking for ways to bind the wounds in that part of the state and, of course, educate local citizens and encourage tourism—that translates to making money! Think about it, son, think about it and pardon the, uh, sermon. Here's the Call—"

"I'm gonna do it. I want to enter that competition," I said. "It will give me a chance to tidy up some loose ends, see Jesse's family, and talk to them about a bunch of stuff." Davenport did not, to my knowledge, know of Jesse as my benefactor or of Skully. I practically snatched the "Call for Entries in Architectural Designs" out of his hands. It may indeed have been a blatant attempt to enter into the Civil War consumer-travel market. *No problem.* For me, it would be a chance to step out of my own shadows and begin carving my name in the contemporary sand.

"Yippee," I said to myself. Truth be told, my education on the western theater of the American Civil War commenced right there in Davenport's office. He gave me one volume he owned on Fort Pillow, *River Run Red* by Andrew Ward, and an article, "*Assessing Civil War Historiography and Nathan Bedford Forrest's Place In It*," by Jonathan GianosSteinberg. He e-mailed me this article which I read with great interest and printed as a bibliographical source, "A

Refutation of Yankee Slanders," *Philologia*, Volume IV, Stephanie Washburn, (https://philologiavt.org/index.php/philologia/article/view/970).

"Caleb, the deadline is in November, so you have three months to come up with something. I can find some money if you want to go down there to look around . . . up to you," said Davenport. "Go down there to see what your ancestors went through on April twelfth of eighteen sixty-four." I decided to swing by Samantha's sorority house to surprise her and tell her of my decision to join with her and visit her personal adviser.

However, Dear Reader, this is where we first met, since my story began at an estate sale, with the exception of that first chapter. I went to the estate sale as a homage to Jesse. I spent pennies and surveyed his books, suspenders, and furniture and loafed about to remember the odor of his pipe, bask in his atmosphere.

A sorority pledge answered the door and said, "Oh, hi, Samantha be out. You're . . . *Tumbleweed* . . . recognize you from the pictures," and the door opened a bit wider. "She got a job for the summer doing catering at the Uptown Grill. She gets off pretty late. Do you want to leave her a note?"

"I should have called, but I wanted to surprise her. I'll call her later," I said and promptly headed

SKULLY

north to the Grill up on Fourteenth Street. It's kinda funny how things can come back to you while walking. I had already started humming, "*To Canaan! To Canaan! The priests and maidens cried: To Canaan! To Canaan! The people's voice replied.*" When you walk the concrete arteries of a city like D.C.—especially when you sniff its varied smells of diesel fuel and the acrid and steel-electric fumes of trolley cars, you realize that there is a sameness about cities wherever you are.

Before I knew it, I stood before the Uptown Grill. I was welcomed by the smell of frying grease and the mildly putrid stench of stale urine. I geared down to slow motion, noticing several young brothers bent into a game of craps in the alleyway. "Sup?" I said, testing the airways for hostile encroachment on my part.

"All you," one answered, giving me a casual glance.

The smell of warm beer started to overtake stench as I walked past several glassy-eyed females and one or two couples, chatting by the side entrance. At the deepest end of the alley, where it met a sharp corner, a lady of medium height—breast exposed—gave me a smile. I tipped my golf cap out of respect and opened the door. Inside, I slowed what had been a modest gait to a full stop. From the jukebox, The Platters crooned a verse of "The Great Pretender." Here and there sat a mix of young and old, the young seeking relief in cool, the old seeking cool in relief. Pausing, I sought the return of eyesight and stood just right of a passageway to the bar. Gradually, I had lost the outdoor smells and found I could see into and past blue smoke.

"Hey, honey," said a waitress, "sit anywhere you want. Need a beer?"

I nodded assent and said, "And some peanuts. Kinda hot outside," and so it was. Perspiration rolled off me, drenching my shirt collar. Now the cooking smells started teasing me; a faint smell of weed mixed with cigarette and cigar smoke and mingled with Willie Nelson singing "Crazy" on a distant radio. I sat at a table, waiting to see if Samantha would appear and drank Miller's from a bottle. Two drunks argued at the bar about the relative merits of the Redskins and how they would fare in the upcoming season. Still no Samantha. I studied the exits, just in case, and picked one of Whitney Houston's tunes on the jukebox, "When You Believe," knowing how much Samantha loved the words. My mood started down a path of reflection, my legs rose from the table, and my feet moved. "Need to go to the restroom—can you get me a burger?"

"No problem," said the waitress, heavily rouged and heavy-hipped. *Maybe coming here was a mistake.*

Shoulda called. I rounded a corner, slowly so as not to run over anyone. *Scope out the joint a bit, get a feel for the place*, said my inner voice.

"I'll put it on your table," said Heavy-Hipped. Inside the john, inner voice spoke again. *Man, this place is a damn disaster. Nothing works. Sticky floor. Full wastebasket. You might want to get your ass outta here.* Towel in hand, I flushed the toilet, exiting opposite the way I came, *tiptoeing* past velvet separators hanging from the ceiling. The smell of weed grew ever so much stronger as I moved deeper into the guts of the building. In midstep, I froze on hearing a long-languishing sigh come into recognition. I put down my foot with unerring delicacy. There it was again, a woman's voice, then a deeper voice—gruff and heavy—"*Take it all, baby*"—spoken in a balanced combination of authority and servitude, laced with tenderness. "*Take it all.*"

"*Oooohhhh,*" preceded an inhale that could only reach ears through clenched teeth. "*Ooohhh, don't—don't take it away.*" The floor-length, black velvet curtains just before me hung from a wooden bar, a foot from the ceiling. Familiar sounds followed familiar passions. I stepped underneath these sounds, followed voices, tailgated the passions. *Is one voice familiar? Yes, perhaps. Be sure. Shoulda called.*

After one bold tiptoe, my sight-line captured

those fabulous golden legs and rump of Sam, arms on the table, back arched convex. Trevor stood behind, brandishing languid strokes with reckless vigor, fingers pinned to her brilliant golden buns, pumping with long, lugubrious strokes similar to those found in the annals of love's—physical love's—ancient porno archives. Behind him, a trusty shotgun, long, black, and shiny, competed—in a gun rack—for the sparky award.

"*Ooooouughhh,*" sang a bleat. Samantha caught my eye as I caught hers. Trevor looked up. Startled, he appeared crumpled, then reached upward as I turned, whipping around in high gear, running toward roomlight, hearing the rack of a shotgun, leaping toward the entry door, hitting the door of the exit and galloping full throttle down the Fourteenth Street corridor. I'd spun and broken into my best running stride and careened against the entry door. The blast struck lumber. I heard a massive tingle of glass, shattered and splintered. My feet never hit pavement as I heard surprised onlookers—some of whom may have been the very folk I had witnessed on my way inside—hollered and cursed. Samantha's face was frozen in my mind, rouged, golden-skinned lips, anguished in full ecstasy, cornered like an alley cat. My mission rested unaccomplished. I exhaled after four blocks and cut through alleyways to reach my apartment. I slept that night with pistol and baseball bat tethered beneath my bed, hurt by my loss but joyful that the truth pierced my eyes. Later that week, I almost sent Sam a text: "Looks like the personal advisor meet is off!"

XX

In short, it appeared that the story of Fort Pillow for the African American soldiers stationed there was *Dipped in Freedom, Dyed in the Promised Land*. I rummaged through various accounts of the short battle listed in several bibliographies and became more fascinated with the contestants. I had yet to read Jesse's obituary and used it as a placeholder for my reading. Being a bit of a skeptic when it comes to things supernatural, I dismissed the whole business of dreams as precursors of doom, but I couldn't help but see that lime-green Chinese dragon as a foreteller of my fate regarding Samantha. For the time being, I kept clear of the frat house and her sorority house, confining myself to organizing sketched copies and photos made in Greece. The battle accounts of Fort Pillow more and more piqued my interest. The drills I'd concocted continued to ease the transfer from theory to muscle to bone. I had three months to get a design accomplished and three weeks before my final year in school commenced.

Lara called to say, "Hey, Mr. 'C.' Most of the news today is about a shooting—a burglary they're calling it—that took place yesterday at the Uptown Grill. Said the suspect hauled butt down Fourteenth Street and disappeared in an alley. You heard anything about that?"

I took a deep breath and countered, "What are you, some sort of detective?"

"That's what forensic psychiatry is all about—detective work," she said adding, "you mentioned Jesse's obituary that your mom gave you. Would you read it to me?"

"Okay," I said, "Jesse Talbot died on July fourth, twenty-seventeen at the age of eighty-two, of natural causes. He was the grandson of a gravedigger and worked for forty-four years at the Government Printing Office. He had no children of his own, but was known for his love and support of children. He enjoyed gardening and was a man of great curiosity. He is survived by two sisters and several nieces and nephews in Memphis, Tennessee. Services will be held on July twelfth, twenty seventeen, ten o'clock at the New Canaan Baptist Church, Wash., D.C."

"You going to be at your apartment for a while?" she said.

"Yep... found some drawings and photos of Fort Pillow. Gonna start sketching some—draw some landscapes of the terrain."

"Okay," said Lara, "I'll be over after I run some errands. If you're thinking about going down to Memphis, include me. I want to see it and get some DNA samples from Jesse's relatives." After hanging up, I dialed Mom.

"I miss Jesse already," Mom said. "He was always asking about you. He and your dad were such good friends. Old friends are starting to tumble into the grave one by one. Pretty soon, there will be no one left. They worked right across the street from each other, Jesse at the post office and your father at the Printing Office, but you know—"

"I miss him too, Mom. He was a good and generous man. It doesn't make me feel any better that I wasn't around—I feel like I should have been here—" I started to tell her about Skully and the gifts but hesitated.

"Don't start with all that, Caleb; you're just beginning, work-wise. You must take advantage of your opportunities when they happen. I understand that. Jesse did too. Use this time to polish talent and build your career base, establish contacts, develop your communication skills. You don't have time to spend with gossipmongers, school truants—only folks that want to help and support forward movement. Speaking of support, what happened to that lovely young lady that brought me to the airport? I like her."

"You mean Lara?"

"Yes, that's the one. She's nice, has a good head on her shoulders."

"Okay, Mom, I'll tell her you asked about her."

My dreams had not bothered me for a while. Though I felt great emotional flux about Skully, my path to solution seemed clear. I had to go see the physical site of Fort Pillow in order to develop a strong design. I hoped to meet the family of Jesse Steward to ask questions about Skully, and I was surprised at the buy-in of Lara. She wanted to make the trip, was great at organizing stuff, and already had monitored Skully's documentation. I no longer felt as though I was hurtling Capitol Domes and was gradually creeping up on Abele's mammoth skill set. I had spoken to Dean Davenport regarding my travel intentions.

"Got your back, son; here's a thousand dollars for a car and motels. Bring in your receipts for gas and food. I'll meet you down there. I want to visit with my sister and see Fort Pillow too; it's been a while since I was there," he said. He gave me crisp bills, lit his cigar, blew a long puff of blue smoke, and danced, with a slight limp, around his desk.

JAMES GHOLSON, JR.

"Whoopee," he shrieked. "*Never* thought I would see this day; got a bud in the Park Service I need to scream at!" I made a meager attempt to return the bills, but he said, "No, no, Caleb—pennies outta my pocket, son. Pennies!"

I had books and printouts spread all over the place—*Dipped in Freedom, Dyed in the Promised Land*. I'd scanned information on the slave codes preceding the Civil War. African American slaves were generally considered three-fifths of a person, could not hold property, were considered chattel, had to carry passes when traveling, could not congregate above double-digits, could not read or learn to read, could not testify against whites in court, and had no rights of self-protection or defense—either in or out of Southern regions. Lara's knock on the door came before I knew it.

"Mornin', everything okay?" I said.

"Great," she said, flashing a smile. "Brought you some breakfast. What's up?"

I explained where I was in readiness for travel and immediately she took out pen and pencil and her smartphone. While I made printouts and text files for reading during travel, Lara made motel and car reservations and contacted Jesse's family. As luck would have it, "They are having a summer theater program in Memphis; their final play is Thursday, and it's about Benjamin Robinson and Louis Napoleon Nelson, two black soldiers in the Civil War. We can catch that easily, if we leave for Memphis tomorrow," said Lara, "Reservations and everything are set to go; let's eat." I was hungrier than I thought.

The following books and articles were in my cardboard travel box: Mainfort, Robert C., *Archaeological Investigations at Fort Pillow, 1976–1978*, Archaeological Div., Tennessee Dept. Conservation, 1976–1978; Turtledove, Harry, *Fort Pillow*, St. Martin's Press, 2006; Fuchs, Richard, *An Unerring Fire*, Stackpole Classics, 2002; Cimprich, John, *Fort Pillow*, L.S.U. Press, 2005; Quinn, Tom, *American Massacre*, CreateSpace, 2014; Bradley, Michael, *Nathan Bedford Forrest's Escort And Staff*, 2006; Wyeth, John A., *Life of Nathan Bedford Forrest*, Harper and Brothers, 1900; Hayes, Benjamin, Without Controversy: The Development of Fort Pillow State Historic Park (Robert Mainfort, "Fort Pillow—letter from L. E. Birchfield)," (benjamin_hayes@nps.gov), 135 Murray Blvd, Suite 100, Hagatna, Guam 96910, Proceedings of the 2011 George Wright Society Conferences on Parks, Protected Areas, and Cultural Sites; and Cimprich, John, and Robert C. Mainfort, Jr., The Fort Pillow Massacre: A Statistical Note. The Journal of American History; Vol. 76, No. 3 (Dec., 1989), pp. 830–837. I also brought along my laptop, loaded with additional PDFs from the Internet Archive.

"Lara, you have been great with helping me get ready to travel again. I feel like I'm stationed in Greece, hovering over D.C., and walking in Memphis. Look, I printed these maps of Memphis and Fort Pillow. There's a ton to see in Memphis—Beale Street, Graceland, Shiloh is on the way, the Civil Rights Museum. It will be tough to get—"

"Not to worry, Caleb, we can cruise by Graceland in the car. Fort Pillow we *have* to see. Jesse's folks are mandatory, and perhaps the Civil Rights Museum. Then there is that play . . . so we will have a full schedule. What time do we leave?"

"Eight sharp," I said.

"I'll be ready."

Lara sat in the back with Skully for the first part of the trip. She wanted to make sure that he was secure and well-protected from lurches, screeches, and hard braking. The thought that I should wear a white shirt and tie while driving South, or that anything untoward could be thought of a young black guy driving through Virginia and Tennessee with a skull in the backseat didn't occur to me until we started driving. I was, at that moment, *acutely* aware of what might be tragically misunderstood! Then, I was especially happy that Lara was riding with us. Lara said,

SKULLY

"Some folks suggest that black guys should wear ties when driving through the South. You ever hear of that?"

"Not really, but I do recall Mom and Dad talking about carrying 'pee' bottles in the car because they could only stop in colored gas stations."

Lara was especially good with Skully and sang verses of "To Canaan" for him. "*What troop is this that follows, All armed with picks and spades? These are the swarthy bondsmen, The iron-skin brigades! They'll pile up Freedom's breastwork, They'll scoop out rebels' graves; Who then will be their owner And march them off for slaves?*"

I'd brought along a CD of the tune. We played it first along I-66, and then I-81. Afterward, we listened to Ward's *River Run Red* as we pursued our sloping route headed toward the Cumberland Plateau. A funny thing happened as we cruised past Bristol. We were getting a bit bleary-eyed and opened windows for fresh air, and we were doing about seventy-two when we heard a strange whistling noise. By then, Lara was sitting in front with me, and we both laughed. The whistling noise was coming from air blowing across the top of Skully's crown. Lara put my Antietam hat on Skully to stop the noise. What a sight! *That's two for Skully fluting; wonder if he was a musician*, I thought.

JAMES GHOLSON, JR.

"Let's stop and eat," said Lara, putting a blanket over Skully and slipping him to the backseat floor.

"Great idea," I said and carefully shuttered the car under shade and locked it. We ate heartily and got on the road within an hour, eyes peeled for Knoxville. Lara sang again to Skully, timing her tempo to the highway lights striking Skully's moonlight-colored, luminous forehead.

To Memphis, To Memphis, To battle for de Lord,
To make ole Massa's backside bleat, and slavery disgorge.

We were positively giddy when we reached Knoxville and ready to call it a day. Lara wrapped Skully up good and tight, and we checked in, took showers. I rolled out my sleeping bag, and we hummed ourselves to sleep ... *To Memphis, To battle for de Lord* ...

XXI

We got on the road early to finish our trip to Memphis. Lara harnessed Skully once more in the backseat, under seat belt, an upturned box, and packing peanuts. She also placed my Antietam slouch hat on him. He seemed quite pleased with himself, almost dashing. While taking the loop around Nashville, I mentioned Fort Negley and the D.C. statue of General George H. Thomas, *The Rock of Chickamauga*. In my rearview mirror, I spied Skully—spinning twice under my hat—while I was driving! Lara was reading on the computer and said, "Check this out . . . After the Fort Pillow *whatever*, the war changed severely in tone. Under no condition would the Confederacy conduct prisoner exchanges of black prisoners; for all intents and purposes, prisoner of war exchanges between the Union and Confederacy ceased. All that suffering at Andersonville and Elmira . . .

JAMES GHOLSON, JR.

Jefferson Davis needed amazing perks to prove his *supposed* superiority."

"From what I've read so far in my research," I said, "some of the few black voices that spoke on the printed page are in the Congressional Investigations and the works of historian George Washington Williams (*A History of Negro Troops in the War of the Rebellion,* 1888). Don't think black folk speak at all on the war in the literature of the Southern historian."

"Betrayed by their own peccadilloes," said Lara. "And this—listen to this—the two hundred and seventy-odd Negro troops at Fort Pillow were there only *eight days,* surrounded by fifteen hundred Rebels and outnumbered—adding the white Union soldiers—*three to one.* Yikes, they had practically no chance at all."

When we passed Shiloh, I nudged Lara to watch Skully before I mentioned Shiloh by name. He never moved a muscle until she turned around to examine the road; then he whistled and blew the hat off through the hole in the top of his head. I pulled off into the next rest stop and asked Lara to drive—felt like I was hallucinating. Lara assumed the wind did it.

"Did I ever tell you about the dream I had, you know, after I fell down the steps at the frat house?"

SKULLY

I said, wondering if I had shared any of my internal stress with her during that period.

"No, not really," she said.

"Well, shortly after that personal trauma," I said, surprised that I could tease myself about it, "I dreamed that I was caught in a rain- and hailstorm—some snow and slush in it too—and somehow ended up caught in tornadic winds, high above the Capitol Dome! I'm cold, it's raining like crazy, wild strikes of lightning unleashed, and I'm sailing above the Capitol Dome and come crashing down into the Potomac River. Waiting for me down there is this huge lime-green Chinese dragon. I wake up just before hitting the water, in a cold sweat. I mean I could see the fire-red tongue and deep into its red and ravenous throat. Truth be told, I felt a bit of exhilaration at the start of that horrendous nose-dive.

"Now, for the last few days, I've been thinking about the slope of my fall. At the frat house it was about 45 degrees. In my dream, that slope had to be at least 80 degrees or more and terrifying. Our trip here from D.C. was about thirty degrees of slope. Now, I say all that to say this: if you look at the drawings, sketches, or pictures—don't have any of those—of the slope of Fort Pillow into the Mississippi, the angles—even at the time of the Civil War—are different! They are both steep and gentle in different places moving north and south on the fort's west side. To me, it seems that the slopes are gentler now than they were in eighteen sixty-four." As I spoke, I thought *Dipped in Freedom, Dyed (Red) in the Promised Land!* "Those guys experienced freedom in free territory for eight days," I said.

"Well, Caleb, that period, that length of freedom time has grown considerably. Guess this is the first time I truly understand their predicament. For them, the choice was existential; there never existed the prisoner option—if caught surrendering, they would not be treated as gentlemen. Hell, black boys now are generally not considered gentlemen. Many have intergenerational reading issues, others warped into themselves and defined by physical ability. Generally, especially at major college institutions, they are adored only for their athletic ability—pure and simple."

We arrived in Memphis a little after three in the afternoon and checked into the Memphis Crowne Plaza Hotel. I cooled out on my sleeping bag. Lara used the time to read a bit and made sure that Skully was well-boxed and safe. Later, after I was awake, she spoke to me about one article she'd read that delved into the politics of Fort Pillow State Park, by Benjamin Hayes. I was a bit surprised at how calmly–almost clinically—she read this excerpt from

Without Controversy: The Development of Fort Pillow State Historic Park.

"Many early historians attempted to frame Fort Pillow *not* as a massacre, but rather a ferocious and unorganized battle in which discipline and control were regretfully lost. One of the most popular Forrest biographies blames the inferior racial intelligence of African-Americans as a reason for higher casualties."

Now that was written a little tongue-in-cheek; the reason—to me, that the entire body of early Southern literature is suspect because blacks rarely speak on those lily-white, magnolia blossom-colored pages—Rebs couldn't abide the documented testimony of blacks in the Congressional Record. After all, blacks weren't supposed to testify against whites according to the rule of law. When she got miffed, Lara really put her back into her reading.

I have to admit that I was surprised by the intensity of her passion. "Hey," I said, "don't get too angry over that stuff—look at how cool and calm old Abele was in his lifetime—and he had family problems—deep wife issues—that could have turned his world upside down."

Lara said, "I know, but when I read some of this, this crap, I get fighting mad." I showed her the map of our trip and said, "Okay, so you're the scientist in this tribe; give me your take on the slope of this hypotenuse between Memphis and D.C. The dean is flying in tomorrow. His sister is picking him up at the airport. Whadaya think? Thirty-five degrees?"

Lara looked, studied the map, and said, "I'd say less than that . . . maybe the teens. We'll ask the dean to comment! It's good that his sister is picking him up, because we have that prayer luncheon with Jesse's family!"

She was elated to be done with the long drive, and I could still hear the hum of the engine as I ferried out bags and paraphernalia up to our room. We'd had a leisurely lunch a little west of Nashville, and were hungry. "You can't go to Memphis and not get some barbecue," Lara's staff cohorts had advised her, so we headed to the first recommendation which Dean Davenport had seconded: The Rendezvous. Memphis presented as a joyful, rambunctious community, and our hotel staffers were helpful in explaining the maps to us and explaining the easiest way to get there. Dean Davenport had paid our bill through Friday, and I didn't feel up to more driving, so we caught a cab after securing Skully in the closet. Sleep came real easy after the meal.

"So glad Dean got single beds; seven solid hours will not be a problem," I said, sinking into well-earned luxury.

SKULLY

"Yep," said Lara, "he knows what a gentleman you are," she said with humor in her voice.

When I awoke, Lara had already grabbed muffins, sausage, and eggs from the lobby and was at my laptop. "Caleb, I got some coffee for you and had an interesting thought last night. I wanted to do some 'pdfgreps' on those digitized PDF files you have of the 1864 Congressional Reports of the Fort Pillow Massacre *and* Returned Prisoners (https://archive.org/details/fortpillowmassac00unit) (https://ia600709.us.archive.org/16/items/fortpillowmassacunit/fortpillowmassacunit.pdf) 'incident,' or whatever they call it down here. Look, see what turns up if you just grep—globally search a regular expression and print—search for 'shot' and 'surrender.' It highlights the words you search for. Interesting how many times those terms turn up in the testimony of the surviving soldiers and the wounded. If I search for 'head'... and add 'shot'..."

$ pdfgrep 'head' fortpillowmassac00unit.pdf
(command line)

(screenshot)
Answer. I was shot twice, and a ball slightly grazed my head.

JAMES GHOLSON, JR.

Answer. I saw them shoot one man in the head after he fell.

Under his head. Some rebels under the hill spied us moving in the brush and me in the head on account of staying there and fighting with the niggers. He ...

Answer. No, sir. I saw one of them shoot a black fellow in the head with three buck shot and a musket ball. The man held up his head, and then the fellow took his pistol and fired that at his head. The black man still moved, and then the fellow took his sabre and stuck it in the hole in the negro's head head soft with it. That was the next morning after the fight.

Crawling along, when a secesh soldier put his revolver to his head, and blew his... not to shoot him, but he drew up his gun and took deliberate aim at his head.

Answer. Yes, sir. While I was in the major's headquarters they commenced ...

"Or this," she said; pdfgrep 'shot' and add 'surrender' fortpillowmassac00unit.pdf

(screenshot)
arm while fighting, shot in thigh after being prisoner, flesh wound, fighting, arm broke, shot in thigh after being prisoner, flesh wound, side and hip after surrender, flesh wound, condition favorable; Sergeant

leg after surrender, flesh wound, favorable; Private Daniel Tylor, company B, Tennessee artillery, shot in right shoulder, shot in right eye after surrender, artillery, shot in left arm after surrender, flesh wound, slight, favorable after surrender, destroying sight, unfavorable Private Alfred shot in left side before, and right arm after surrender, flesh wound, serious, in head and right arm after surrender, causing fracture of ann, condition after surrender, wound serious, condition unfavorable; Private Charles D, 1st Alabama artillery, shot in right arm after surrender, fracture of

Fintis, company D, 1st Alabama artillery, shot in both legs after sur- B, 1st Tennessee artillery, shot in left side of head, shot in right wrist after nessee artillery, shot through nose after surrender, not serious, condition amputation, shot in left arm, fracture of arm after surrender, very unfavorright side of head after surrender, not serious,

JAMES GHOLSON, JR.

favorable; Private Thomas Gadis, company C, 1st Alabama artillery, shot in right hip after surrender, shot in right leg while fighting, shot in left arm after surrender, flesh in right thigh and arm after surrender, flesh wound, condition favorable; Nathan Modl'ey, Company D, 1st Alabama artillery, shot in right knee after pany B, 1st Tennessee artillery, shot in right thigh after surrender,

"That's the kind of forensic work that was not done in the moment, Caleb. So many of these fellas were *shot* at close range in the *head*. Much more so than you would find in a normal battle. One day, someone will do linguistic tests on the testimony and those tests will add to the quality of truth that already exists. Some politicians are uncomfortable with that. Tough!" I was fascinated by her intuitive leap and tried a few words myself: "surrender," "shot," "head"—all with resulting snippets of the testimony of individual Federal soldiers.

While Lara took her shower, I ran the pdfgrep test with "testimony" on this pdf, *Life of Lieutenant-General Nathan Bedford Forrest by Wyeth*, John A. (John Allan), 1845–1922; Duke, Basil Wilson, 1838–1916. Negro testimony was also the focal point of *The Campaigns* of *General Forrest*, Thomas Jordan, BLELOCK & CO., 1867., rendering no data on

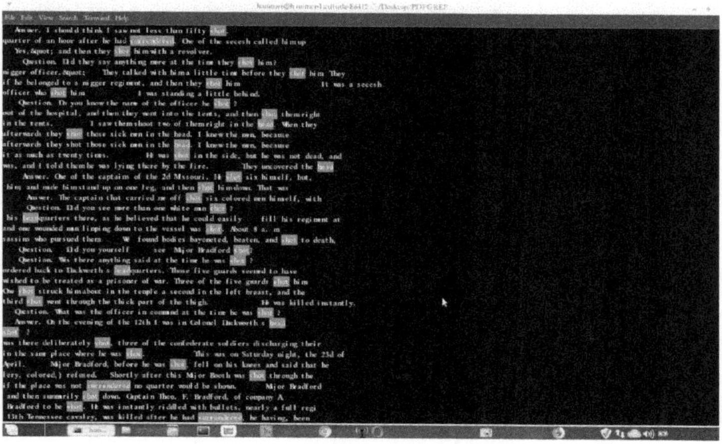

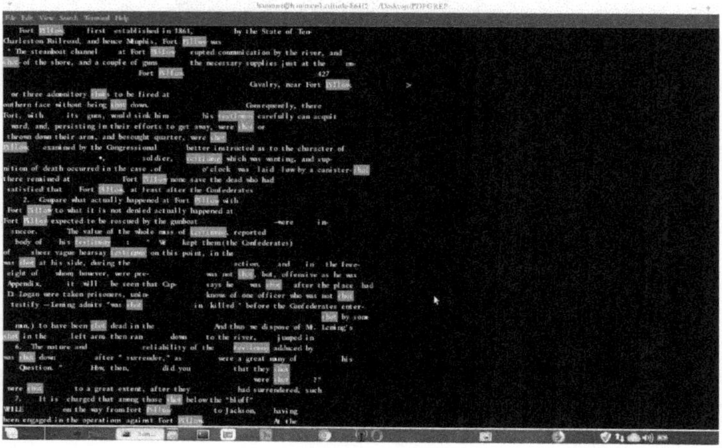

JAMES GHOLSON, JR.

"surrender," "shot," "head"—in the chapter on Fort Pillow (pp 424, abj6714.0001.001.umich.edu.pdf).

> (screenshot)
> bear *testimony* to Forrest s harshness and violent temper should General Gideon J. Pillow reported the sworn *testimony* of Cap 3000 men & quot;* The *testimony* of a number of men who escaped to the saddle. It was the universal *testimony* of the men that *testimony* to the dilapidated condition of the Federal command while it is the general *testimony* of the survivors among the Consary of the fort was supplied. The sworn *testimony* of a large their official report. There is sworn *testimony* that some two enforced the order. Among the mass of sworn *testimony* which Major-General Hurlbut should declare in his *testimony* before the deftly woven out of the exaggerated *testimony* of two or three of garrison, much of which *testimony* was so self-contradicting as to have deemed it proper to take some *testimony* in reference to the *testimony* of these Union officers shows that the women volume of sworn *testimony* in the writers possession shows pos study the *testimony* and believe they were), they could only have battle. Their *testimony* says that & quot;

The *testimony* of a number of other witnesses who ..were on the and that the *testimony* of certain witnesses made before the sub... 12, 1864. That the *testimony* of certain witnesses made before the very last firing done at Fort Pillow, ...the *testimony* of certain witnesses.. port that the universal *testimony* of rebels, officers and men, is...

"I wonder . . ." said Lara when she had finished . . . "if Skully comes from Fort Pillow!"

Almost as if a chorus we said, "Damn!"

"That may be why Jesse was protecting it—if he knew that—and we are going to be late to the luncheon," said Lara. I munched a muffin, scooped up some eggs, and took a quick shower. She'd already had hers and had Skully packed up—and we each dressed to head to the luncheon. "That is the kind of forensic work that was *not* done at Fort Pillow."

In a quiet voice, Caleb said, "The Confederates did not provide detailed and comprehensive interviews of their troops at Fort Pillow—never did."

"Forensic work like this fascinates me, especially with the leaps available now in technology, Caleb; and the fields—linguistics, ground-penetrating radar, psychology too," said Lara as I drove.

I said, "Wyeth attacked the *testimony* of black and white soldiers, miles apart, in different places, different times; he resented black *testimony*—as did Anderson; plus, Wyeth wasn't there. Forrest's report never mentions *how* the soldiers were killed, never mentions the word *surrender*, nor does Barteau's. Basically, Wyeth did a bait and switch and attacks the word 'testimony.' He did not challenge the facts as reported in Congressional documents."

"Excited" is not the word for how I felt. Memphis had been ground zero for so many historic personalities and events—Ida Wells, Martin King, Fort Pillow—that to experience it firsthand was a treat.

Davenport called after landing to say hello. I thanked him for paying for our accommodations. He said, "Meet you at Fort Pillow in the morning. It's a pleasure to fund this project, my pleasure! See you in the morning." Lara had all the scientific documentation she'd collected from Skully's various examinations, and we arrived in short order, with the help of GPS, in a place called Whitehaven, at the home of Mose, Jesse's cousin. Jesse's sisters Aubrey and Sissy were already there.

Lara wanted to do the honors. She said, "Mose, Sissy, and Aubrey, it's a pleasure to give you Skully. I checked Skully's DNA against Jesse's already from his coffee cup: *no relation*. Caleb here was presented with Skully by Jesse in the late winter. We are returning him to Jesse's family; we think he would want you to have him. Jesse wanted him buried in free soil, where Skully is loved and honored. We know you guys can provide that for him. He was in good health at the time of death, comes from a West African country according to DNA results, and we think—"

Sissy, Jesse's sister, interrupted. "Let me tell you a story. When I married, I jus' couldn't stand to have that skull in the house. I mean, dude is creepy and whistles when left in a draft—he sings! I gave him to Jesse, and he took it to D.C. Our great-grandfather found that skull up at Fort Pillow—he was a gravedigger—when they transferred the soldiers originally interred there to the National Veterans Cemetery. Since then, many visitors—kids playing and others—have found skulls and human skeletal fragments at the fort. You call him Skully? Well, old Skully has been in the family for one hundred and fifty years. Jesse took him to D.C. years ago, along with silverware from great-granddaddy's stuff, family hand-me-downs, and such.

"Jesse collected antiques at estate sales too; Daddy was amazed at his gift for antiques. I wrote a chapter or so on Fort Pillow—tried to imagine what Pillow was like. Sent Jesse a copy. Our great-granddad said he saw loose bones and skulls when he got up there and hated their mistreatment after they had given up life itself in the fight for freedom."

JAMES GHOLSON, JR.

"The least we can do is to honor their remains," Mose said. "That was in eighteen sixty-seven or eight, I believe. Jesse was up there jus' tryin' to keep his promise to Granny, though he may have guessed her intention was to keep that warrior safe," said Mose.

"We thank you greatly on his behalf," said Sissy.

Mose was a preacher and said a short prayer before we ate. "Lord, even as this terrible atrocity—a pagan ritual—happened close to Easter, we forgive the perpetrators of these crimes of humanity, their trespass on the rules of war." He added, "We honor the Passion and Resurrection of our dear Savior Jesus Christ during that time, with joy, festivities, and commitment to the Golden Rule, to the human race on earth. God bless beloved Jesse, keep him in our hearts and minds, and thank you for his friends and the privilege of remembering Skully and his well-earned rest. Amen!" And we had more barbecue; this time it was chicken.

XXII

"Ain't no lawyer, but those Southern Codes were truly a bitch!" said Dean Davenport, looking inside a large, heavy carrying bag and making adjustments to something inside it. "Free persons of color were exempted from military duty—mind you, they did everything they could to keep slaves unarmed—free men of color still were restricted in their right to testify against a white man." The dean had met us in our hotel lobby.

"Well, we'll be in a National Park, so we should be okay," said Lara, munching on a sausage biscuit. I was trying to keep my eyes on the road without cracking up on their childish banter.

"Now the slave was disallowed by law to testify against whites, debarred from the benefits of education and self-defense, and denied the ordinary safeguards of trial by jury. Bet 'chall didn't know that!" Davenport said, his eyes twinkling playfully, drinking

JAMES GHOLSON, JR.

in the beautiful countryside. A pickup truck sailed past us, its Rebel flag flapping billows of dust, clouding our path. We'd passed through Henning and upcoming on the left was the Fort Pillow prison.

"Now y'all be good'uns or you'll end up over yonder," he said teasing Lara yet again, as we passed the Fort Pillow Penitentiary. "Been all through these woods as a youngster never knowing what the fuss was all about 'til being released into academia." He laughed a big bold belly laugh. "Jeff Davis would love to see y'all behind bars, 'specially if you were caught with a gun. States-rights prevailed, and they were real tough on darkies caught with guns. All the shootin' going on nowadays, he woulda had himself a field day!"

A park ranger got us started on our tour with a movie and somebody asked about the contraband camp that had been set afire at the onset of the Fort Pillow attack. The ranger responded, saying, "Early on, around 6:00 a.m. as far as we know, all children and women, white and contraband, were reportedly removed. They ran into the fort and were subsequently ferried to a small island that existed out in the middle of the river."

Every report that I read had accounts of Chalmers shooting one boy that a Confederate was trying to save from annihilation. Apparently, Davenport noticed

SKULLY

this also; a bizarre frown wiggled across his brow.

"Early on at about 6 a.m., the Union pickets had been driven in. General Anderson initiated Forrest's pincer movement—a military offensive grapple—to surround the fort, with McCullough on the left, Bell in the center, and Barteau on the right, to surround the fort short of the crescent-shaped gully that you see encircling it.

"Reports say that Forrest arrived about 10:00 a.m. and took over all responsibility for the fort's investment. The commanding officer, Lionel Booth, of Fort Pillow, was killed at 9:00 a.m. by a sharpshooter's bullet," said the ranger.

I was still steaming inside from the sugar-coated answer in response to the question about contraband—I preferred to use black *refugees*—not contraband—which had been used in the recent past to define whiskey, and most recently, cannabis, or weed. Clearly, contraband *refugees* were in a war zone, caught in the midst of full-out Civil War hostilities between the North and the South.

"Long-arms were used in the initial attack," said the ranger, "as the Confederates generally eschewed the use of sabers. Forrest liked revolvers and six-shot pistols, recognizing that sabers were noisy and ineffective in fighting at close range. Robert Mainfort, who conducted archaeological investigations in 1976,

JAMES GHOLSON, JR.

found bullet fragments from a Whitworth rifle, a crucial Rebel military instrument. It was deadly accurate from distances over the length of three football fields." The ranger read from a battle report, "My command consisted of McCulloch's brigade, of Chalmers's division, and Bell's brigade of Buford's division, both placed for the expedition under the command of Brig. Gen. James R. Chalmers, who, by a forced march, drove in the enemy's pickets. Critical to the attack was the defender's inability to rake the slopes."

Immediately, upon hearing "rake the slopes," I thought *Tumbleweed* and imagined Rebels being picked off like grapes in a vineyard perched high above the breastworks. In actuality, Union soldiers could not mount the breastworks of Fort Pillow as sharpshooters positioned on several knolls could easily pick them off. My imagined perception was pure folly.

Forrest's men, "gained position on the slopes (knolls) where our men would be perfectly protected from heavy fire of their artillery . . . nor could they fire on them without mounting the breastworks and exposing themselves to the fire of our sharpshooters . . ." Davenport stood behind the ranger, making faces and V signs. That *Devil Forrest* moniker teased my mind—I gulped. The woman next to me chuckled.

"11:00 am: The Confederates made a determined

charge on the fort," said the ranger, "which was repulsed; however, the artillerists inside the fort could not fire into the depths of the ravine. By this time, Union forces were commanded by inexperienced Major Bradford. James Bingham, a white civilian defender, watched worried black soldiers, 'With blood running from their bodies, still engaged loading and firing canon and musket cheerfully.' One of the barracks had been burned about 9 a.m., after a desperate struggle in and around those premises. Some sources mention taunts and the drinking of liquor by black soldiers; this allegation has not been substantiated. Shells lobbed at the Confederates, from the New Era gunboat on the Mississippi, appear to have been largely ineffective.

"Chalmers's force was strung out in a line similar to Fort Pillow's crescent, and to the right of McCulloch's. While conducting reconnaissance, Forrest had several horses shot out from under him. Major Bradford sent troops to burn the barracks, which stood at a vantage point visible to artillerists. Guess what? If they could see the Rebels, the Confederates could see them. Federals were able to torch *only one row* of barracks, giving the Confederate forces of Anderson and McCulloch clear and direct sight lines to Federal skirmishers and artillerists, *inside the fort*. Any questions?"

JAMES GHOLSON, JR.

Dean Davenport stood behind the ranger and, mouth wide open, rolled his eyes upward toward the heavens. I stood directly across from the ranger. *What happened to the folks at the contraband camp?* Whilst in my absentminded reverie, Davenport had trotted up to the southern entrance of the fort, taken out a drone, and had that drone circling about the south-westernmost slopes of the fort, him trotting over hill and dale giggling like a kid. He was joined by Lara, who skipped about taking pictures.

The unsuspecting ranger continued. "Colonel Barteau had taken some time in placing his Second Regiment in the northern portion of the ravine, protected by a heavy body of sharpshooters on the hills and knolls. Post-Civil War, both General James Chalmers and Colonel Barteau became lawyers in Memphis, with Chalmers serving in Congress." *Jeez, probably helping to legitimize the Jim Crow era.*

"At about three o'clock, Forrest issued a call for surrender. Debate centers around whether he moved troops during this parlez for surrender. Confederates argue that he feared approaching gunboats and moved troops toward the landing area to keep soldiers from landing (by boat) and mitigate their influence. Federals say that this movement was a violation of the rules of warfare. Having escaped Fort Donelson early in the war, Forrest was faced with a call for

'Unconditional Surrender,' by U.S. Grant. Forrest adopted this technique—which was not original with him—to use in many of his military contests."

Fingers circling around his head, Davenport, I would later find out, had—to a large degree—dismissed the veracity of the park ranger. Later, Davenport would say, "A mere child whom an officer had taken up behind him on his horse was seen by Chalmers, who brusquely ordered him to put the kid down and shoot him."

"Major Bradford, commanding officer after the death of Lionel Booth, refused Forrest's offer of surrender," said the ranger. "Some accounts of the battle say the Confederates used the period of truce negotiations to further surround the fort, especially on its south side; others say that Forrest was checkmating any ships that threatened to land in the area."

"3:00: Forrest is resupplied with ammunition and issues an order for surrender at this time, warning the Federals of imminent assault. Between four-thirty and five o'clock, the bugler sounded the charge, and Fort Pillow was taken by storm between 4:30 and 5:00. At the time of the breach, Federals broke, running down the slopes of Fort Pillow through a murderous cross-fire and botched retreat. Soldiers of the Tennessee 13th Cavalry would later say that the black soldiers were first to break and run; black

JAMES GHOLSON, JR.

soldiers would say the Tennessee Cavalry first broke and ran. Lt. Mack Lemming testified later, 'Then followed a scene of cruelty and murder without a parallel in civilized warfare, which needed but the tomahawk and scalping-knife to exceed the worst atrocities ever committed by savages.' This carnage that followed has been documented in an array of books written about this unfortunate *affair*," said the ranger.

"Robert Mainfort, author of *Archaeological Investigations at Fort Pillow*, used the *letters* and *diaries* of Confederate soldiers as primary resources, in asserting that a massacre did take place. The artifacts found here, located after one hundred and fifty years of metal detecting and relic searches, were used to pinpoint troop locations and verify presence. The fort was stormed shortly thereafter; the controversy on events happening after the fort was stormed is yet a point of debate, with contemporary historians—using statistical data, documents, and primary testimony—leaning toward the theme of massacre. John Cimprich's article, 'Fort Pillow: A Statistical Note,' is particularly insightful from a statistical point of view. Mainfort's research documents are located at the University of Arkansas Libraries (mc1667). Thank you for your attention, ladies and Gentlemen. Are there any questions?"

The ranger hobnobbed with several visitors, taking pictures and explaining portions of his talk. He was a tall, angular man who in some ways reminded me of Abe Lincoln. Davenport—whom I had always seen as reserved, a muted academic in demeanor and impeccably dressed—chased the mercurial movements of his drone this way and that. Occasionally he dipped below the horizon, his torso floating, as if on a Segway, cruising and bumping across the landscape as if he knew the place for the first time! Lara merrily gazed upon the sight happy to see, "He's having a grand time!" I must admit that I was woefully embarrassed by his actions.

Dean Davenport's sister Constance showed up at one thirty with a picnic basket. I knew she was related to him, as she looked exactly like him about the face, though she was a bit taller than the dean.

"Look over yonder at that poor puppy; he's lost his mind again," Constance said laughing. "Lemme tell you, Caleb, Herman hasn't ferried himself around like that since he was a boy! He got that limp he has from a snakebite. Came down to this very place, saw bones himself out in the water, tried to fetch 'em, failed, and got bit by a snake right as Daddy yanked him out of there. Had to hightail it down to Memphis to save that leg!"

I took out a sketch pad and made pencil sketches

JAMES GHOLSON, JR.

of the knolls and slopes. "Son, don't let any place get you down," said sister Constance. "Most believe there was a massacre here—an awful, *terrible* thing. Benjamin Hayes gets it about right. I'll send you a copy of that article. I've seen many black folk rant and rave, break down, get pissed off—cry, even. Dean there used to get that-a-way. That's why he brings a joy stick—this time a doggone *dron*e—with him, most anywhere. For him, it's his personal *yo-yo*—an *emotional* gyroscope. He can point his angles and slopes high or low, left or right—any trajectory that he wants at the time; get yourself a yo-yo and keep it in your pocket. Aim it high, slope it up to the stars in memory of the massacred at Fort Pillow. Keeps things light and bubbly—air-bound, he calls it!"

Davenport was tuckered out after chasing that drone; at times he appeared as an overweight, jolly jackrabbit! "Whew, haven't had that much fun in years. What kinda sandwiches we got, sis?"

Lara now just sat and looked, taking in the beauty of the place.

"You know, you can find the history of this place—the emotional history—in the art of Pollack and Basquiat—our great abstract expressionists. I put Abele right up there with those guys. Think about the Scopes Trial and this battle of hills, bad angles, and horrid slopes for the black Federals . . . Scopes and slopes! We still hear the battle cries of Fort Pillow in the streets of Chicago, Watts, D.C.—*died free*," said Davenport.

"Pillow is the place where the gun preceded education—reading, writing—the jewels and benefits of Western culture. Drones, infrared technology, magnetic imaging, all the new archaeological technologies may never see this place. After all, the Scopes Trial pitted science against religious folklore in this very state. Guess which one won? *Incivility* trumps the pearls of the West! Then came refusals to fully engage blacks with one hundred and fifty years of Jim Crow—*legally* blocked from civility.

"Blacks folk have broken through as individuals here and there, but many yet wade in the waters of poverty and poor education. And we watch symphonies, galleries, museums languish, poorly supported; mostly they don't get that communication is a two-way street. That's how we got to this ugly monster of a leader—our consummate Ugly American—Michener is rolling over in his grave. Our black leadership is no longer quick and nimble . . . probably don't talk to each other. Stop me if I'm lecturing," he said.

"Stop, Herman, you're lecturing," said his sister, adding, "so, what's the plan? Today is Tuesday; tomorrow, you kids are on your own. Gonna take Sonny back to Brownsville with me. We'll come down and take you guys to dinner and the play. Here's my telephone number; call us if anything comes up." We parted with hugs and thank yous.

"So, Lara," I said, "do you mind if I sketch for an hour, and then we'll head back to Memphis?"

"Go for it, Caleb, sketch your slopes. I'm headed to the bookstore."

XXIII

In Their Own Words
Program Notes
A Virtual Conversation:

Witness a dialogue between two soldiers, veterans of the Civil War era, about their motivations for fighting in that war. Generally, blacks were unable to testify in court against a white person in the American South by the *eighteen fifty law*. At the time, James Seddon, Confederate Secretary of War, intoned these words:

"The foundation of the Southern theory of racial superiority of whites would crumble if blacks were allowed to enlist." Alexander Stephens echoed the same philosophy in his "Cornerstone" speech . . . "the Confederacy's 'cornerstone' rests upon the great truth, that the Negro is not equal to the White man; that slavery—subordination

JAMES GHOLSON, JR.

to the superior race—is his natural and normal condition."

Scene:
Two African American soldiers sit on stage. One, in a butternut-gray uniform, stands behind a large kettle and stirs a ladle, as if cooking. The other sits in a chair, whittling a long stick—perhaps a toy rifle—as he rocks back and forth in his chair. He wears a uniform of navy blue. Both men are of advanced years, and both are somewhat gray. Behind the soldiers stands a group of teenage boys and girls; they have quietly marched in columns of threes and are dressed in long, white robes.

Narrator: (Sissy Steward)
"Good evening, Gentlemen, welcome to *In Their Own Words*. We are honored to be in your presence and are most thankful for your service. Our audience appreciates the opportunity to witness your presence and commentary. We want to know who you are and why you fought in the Civil War. Let me read a portion of this earlier narrative; it comes from manuscript pages I sent to my brother some time ago. We read about Fort Pillow penned by an old friend, a great, great old man whom we knew long ago.

SKULLY

"... The place sloped into the river in multiple guises; some slopes were almost ninety degrees into the water, others more gentle like the one into the landing dock. All slopes ended in the Mississippi. They came to the place up a slope sometimes befitting a hill and at other points, a bluff, to join the Tennessee 13th Cavalry..."

"... Meanin' we get to do it," said Sandy. Rain drizzled less hard on the thin tin which shielded the fire from extinction. Nearby, they could hear the bugler doing his warm-up routine: buzzing on the mouthpiece. Now and then, the firewood popped, crackling against the fall of casual raindrops.

"But you know—sure you know dis already—there are some folk, black folk, that are believin' on the rebels. Now, how you figure on dat?" said Dan.

"Dun' heard dat one too; takin' their chances on de Confederates winnin'. Old Tubman dun' said already, 'Saved a thousand slaves to freedom and coulda saved a thousand mo', if'n dey knew dey were slaves.' I figure they wait to see which way fortunes break; smart really. Fortunes break at different times for different folk. Don' git no mo' confusin' den dat. Gonna turn in; sleep tight; dey gon' blow taps any minute." Ben tugged at his rain slick, tightening it around his chest, and headed for his tent. For a strange reason, his palms felt sweaty. Was there reason to be nervous? He wondered and fell asleep before the notes of taps came to an end . . .

Ben: (Ben Robinson)
"Ah grew up in South Carolina as a slave and was sold to a plantation owner in Jackson, Mississippi. Ah escaped from there to join the Union in Corinth and become promoted to sergeant of the Sixth U.S. Colored Heavy Artillery Regiment 'ventually stationed at Fort Pillow. I fought to gain my freedom, pure and simple. Us boys was talking things over right before the fort was attacked; talking about how the breastworks was too thick to allow movement of the cannon, so's to hit low objects outside the fort—come to think of it, wasn't no abatis 'stablished anywheres around either. Mentioned it to my supervisor—said we'd get to it."

Louis: (Louis Napoleon Nelson)
"I'se raised right here close to Memphis on de

plantation of E. R. Oldham, yessuh. When him and his son joined the war, I'se gone as his bodyguard. We be all dere togetha, to protect de homeland, our property on't, and our families from invasion by Yankees. I'se joined up as a cook and gradual become a chaplain in the ranks of de Rebels under Forrest. Yessuh, started out foraging, cookin', and dem boys loved my preachin' so much dey just had to have me speak to 'em on the Bible. Folks asked me many a time if I'se owned a gun. How kin you forage widout a gun? Course I'se had a rifle—knew how to use it!"

Chorus: (*in unison*)
What troop is this that follows,
All armed with picks and spades?
These are the swarthy bondsmen,—
The iron-skin brigades!

Narrator:
"Well, Ben, you were at Fort Pillow. What did you see?"

Ben:
"Well, we fought hot and heavy from 'bout six in de mornin'. Remember my thigh'd be twitchy de night before, and massaged it right quick. De

secesh charged us twice, at nine and eleven, while de New Era, down on de Mississippi, lobbed shot and cannon canister at dem from out on de river. Each time de New Era fired, de secesh would move out of one ravine into anuder. Major Booth was shot in de heart, right next to me, and Bradford took over, making sure folk were staying focus'd, rallying de troops. I served on de gun crew commanded by Michael Carron. De black soldiers wuz all fightin' fo' our lives; we ain't put no truck in prisoner-of-war talk. Later found out we wuz out-numbered three to one; in de moment, figured it was fight to de death. Come dis far to Canaan, de Promised Land, wasn't 'bout to turn around."

Louis:
"Well, I'se weren't up at Fort Pilla . . . weren't assigned to that trip though General Chalmers wuz dere. He never spoke to me on Pilla directly, but you could tell de gen'rals wuz real worked up 'bout it on account of what de papers said—massacre of ruthless butchery—they called it 'n dat fired up Forrest pretty good. Anderson too. Tell de truth 'bout it, me and Forrest sounded real similar, both being from de old South. Forrest being de slave trader dat he wuz, spoke and sounded

lak he *wuz* one—a slave, dat is. Anderson wrote all his reports and memos and orders. Forrest din't write any o' dat stuff. Young Willis Howcott wuz up 'ere, though, and we spoke on it. He say de Federals got whupped somethin' awful—shot down lak dogs and pigs in a nigger yard. Me, I'se be in Oxford."

Chorus:
What Captain leads your armies
Along the rebel coasts?
The Mighty One of Israel,
His name is Lord of Hosts!

Louis:
"Wait a minute, did want to add that I'se memorized de Good Book, de Bible, early on. Forrest be glad to have me—boys too—called me Uncle Louis and delivered prayers all over yonder, and for Forrest forty slaves. We called 'em de teamster brigade, 'cuz Forrest promised 'em their freedom aftah de war's end."

Ben:
"We had a chaplain also, but he sure didn't know de Bible so well. Ah reckon he should have prayed with the 13th Cavalry a little more, 'cause

humility was not their strong suit. Looked to me like they spent too much time grooming horses and not enough time helping to prepare that fort for serious defense. First thing Forrest's men did was to steal de horses and take 'em to safe ground. That's right after he done drove the pickets in."

Chorus:
To Canaan, to Canaan
The Lord has led us forth,
To blow before the heathen walls
The trumpets of the North!

Narrator: "Well, Uncle Louis, why did you fight for the Confederacy?"

Louis:
"Why did I'se fight for de Confederacy? Dat's an easy one. Everybody knows dat dem invaders were on de way from de North. Comin' to take our property, mules, guns, houses, children ad womens too. Damn Yankee invaders foragin' and plunderin' through Memphis. Hell, dey burnt Randolph down to de ground! Dat was Sherman's doin'; it wuz mine devine 'sponsibility to protect my master and his son. Ah was determined to save us all from de Yankees and preserve my

hard work! Course, I wanted to please my master; d'otherwise, I'se be a mighty sad slave—no house, no children, no wife, no mule. What good freedom if'n you ain't got nuttin'. Anderson done 'splained to me dat Seddon won't auta-rise arm de slaves—Forrest too, so Ah fire guns *onliest* to forage and in dire 'mergencies, only den!"

Ben:
Ah figure you ain't got nuttin' anyway, not even your own children if they can be sold out from under you any old time. Felt to me like I didn't even own myself. So Ah be determined to do just that, buy myself, own myself, fight for myself, *free* myself. We were free when we signed up, and the boys at that fort who died in bloody waters nd dry land, were dyed red and died free. Freedom may not have lasted that long, but dey made the journey to the Promised Land and breathed air as freemen.

Chorus:
In many a battle's tempest
It shed the crimson rain,—
What God has woven in his loom
Let no man rend in twain!

JAMES GHOLSON, JR.

Narrator:

As Forrest *(Anderson)* himself wrote, "The river was dyed with the blood of the slaughtered for 200 yards. It is hoped that these facts will demonstrate to the Northern people that Negro soldiers cannot cope with Southerners." I might add that of the soldiers stationed at Fort Pillow, thirty-one (31) percent of the white soldiers were killed as opposed to sixty-four (64) percent of the black soldiers killed (Cimprich, John, and Robert C. Mainfort Jr. *The Fort Pillow Massacre: A Statistical Note* 76(3) (1989): 830–837. http://www.jstor.org/stable/2936423).

Table 3		
Federal Casualties by Unit (High Estimate for Bradford's Battalion)		
White	Black	Total
Died 102 (34%)	195 (64%)	297 (49%)
Lived 198 (66%)	110 (36%)	308 (51%)
Total 300 305 605		
Note: $X2 = 54.22$, $df = 1$, $p < .oOl$; $4 = .30$		
The new quantitative and documentary evide nce unequivocally demonstrates that a massacre occurred.		

Narrator:

"Why do you think that happened?"

Ben:
"Well, strange things happen in the heat of battle. Ah seen secesh shoot two white men right by the side of me after they had laid their guns down. They shot one black fella clear over in the river. To me, they said, 'give me your money, you damn nigger.' Ah told them Ah did not have any. Ah was shot about three o'clock after Ah had surrendered. They shot pretty much everybody after they had surrendered. I saw no secesh officers trying to stop them. Wiley saw rebel officers; said the officer told secesh to kill us all. They had a clear line of fire into the fort, once they had possession of the cabins. Tom Alison pleaded with Bradford and the officers to burn the cabins early on, but they waited too long to order it done. Just read that letter, written by Achilles Clark . . . wrote his sisters that Forrest ordered us shot down like dogs."

Louis:
"Well, I'se knowed that Chalmers and Forrest were not happy wid Bradford and aimed to ferret him out. Furstest, they got plenty requests for help from Jackson, Tennessee. They had a tough time up at Paducah; don' had a whole wheelbarrow of niggers up thar, fightin' for de

JAMES GHOLSON, JR.

Federals, and got whipped up pretty bad! Kinda wished I'se coulda been dere to say prayers over de dead. Dey should knowed better'n to fight agin' de massa. Lak I'se said, Howcott was up thar, and he say it was a terrible, terrible sight. Said some chil'rens and womenfolk got caught up in the fray and kilt. Lotta niggers shot in de haid all over de place. Mostest, Genr'l Forrest be pissed wid de newsprint coverage of Fort Pilla, yessah. I'se memorized de King James Version of de Good Book *but can't read a lick.* On his return, he took a meal in de tent and say, 'Uncle Louis—speak to de Lawd and come pray ovah me in my tent—and I'se did . . . (Uniformed in Confederate gray, the tall General Forrest enters, kneels, and Louis stands over him—hand on his shoulder—and speaks, 'Our Father, who art in heaven . . .'"

The lights dim and the actors leave the stage.

Chorus:
To Canaan, to Canaan
The Lord has led us forth,
To sweep the rebel threshing-floors,
A whirlwind from the North.

The Chorus leaves the stage singing "To Canaan," a Union marching song.

Narrator:
"Thank you, Ladies and Gentlemen, for your attention! Good night."

XXIV

Dean Davenport and his sister met us in the lobby of the Crowne Plaza after the play was over. "It's so nice to meet you both," said Constance, "you and your lovely Lara. My brother thinks so much of you and appreciates your character and industry, Caleb. Hold on to all that silverware Jesse gave you; get it appraised sometime soon. Lara told me about it. Take care of her and be careful driving back to D.C. I'm taking Herman to the airport in the morning, so we'd better get going." The dean smiled, and we all exchanged hugs.

"I hope to get back one of these days," I said, walking them to their car. Lara disappeared to the elevator saying, "Good night and thanks for a great time!" Dean handed me a small box containing a yo-yo as he departed and said, "This is your drone substitute; never lose that sense of play," he said laughing, "and stop by when you get back."

A single candle burned when I stepped inside our room, and Lara sat on the side of the bed staring at me. When I fumbled for the light switch, she said, "I cut it off on purpose."

"Oh," I said and sat beside her, taking off my shoes before heading to my quarters.

"I have something I want you to see," she said.

In my mind, I was already sketching and sculpting a rash of new ideas which had come to me during the play, many of them versions of Abele's "Exedra" executed at Haverford College in Philadelphia. In the elevator, I had imagined Nelson and Robinson seated at the exedra portal, discussing their separate rationales for choosing to join their respective armies.

"Okay," I said somewhat belatedly, "what's up?" In my pocket, I reached for the program on which I had sketched in the dark, some preliminary models based on Abele's work. She hugged me from the rear as I'd turned to move my shoes under my "quarters," and gave me a kiss on the back of my neck. I could feel her arms trembling.

"Lara, you are trembling like a leaf," I said, and when I got to the "f" part of *leaf,* her lips were on mine. I coasted backward, relaxing to break my fall off the bed ... but my fall never happened!

"Had to keep you from falling; you almost crushed the thing I wanted to show you!" she said.

JAMES GHOLSON, JR.

"In the afterglow of candlelight, it's kinda hard to see behind you," was my report, adding, "It's a—tent?"

"No, silly, it's a pillow-fort—I put the beds together. This is our last night in Memphis, and I want to have a little party with you." Lara handed me a plate of scallops and fried rice, along with a cold Modelo beer. I kissed her back her several times, enjoying the touch of her smooth skin and hair. Arms around her, it was hard to not notice the intense firmness of her nipples—every bit as hard as my lower anatomy; to tell the truth, we made love all the way to D.C.

Dean was effusive about how much he enjoyed his trip. He had wonderful images and videos of Fort Pillow, especially the slopes, in angles both small and tall. "I loved running around in Fort Pillow—Remember Fort Pillow!—and finally got some sort of composure with the place. Connie enjoyed meeting you guys. If you ever need room and board for free when you're there, call her." He showed me the yo-yo he kept in his desk drawer, "as a pleasant distraction, used when you are too mad to think!"

Arabelle had done some research of her own on the staff and escort of Nathan Bedford and added, "General Chalmers and Colonel Barteau became lawyers in Memphis and, no doubt, helped to usher in the Jim Crow Era. I found this piece on Forrest in the *Morning Star and Catholic Messenger, May 12,*

1878. The Fort Pillow Massacre. It was a bit after he captured Fort Pillow, and as so much has been said about his 'ruthless butchery' of the garrison there."

"I will give my recollection of his own statement to me about it. I said to him one day: 'I hear you shot some of your own men at Fort Pillow; how was that?'"

"Well," he (Forrest) said, "I'll tell you how that was. The boys had promised their wives and sweethearts to bring them a calico frock the first chance they got at a Yankee store, and while we were fighting our way up to the breastworks of Fort Pillow, I noticed the firing ceased all at once on the left side of my line, and so I rode down that way to see what was the matter, and as I rode up, one of the boys came out with his arms full of dry goods. I was so mad I dropped him with my pistol; right behind him came another, and he was a captain, and he too was loaded with plunder, and I shot him as well.

"They all went on with the fighting after that."

"Well," I said, "how about your shooting the Negroes after they had surrendered?"

"Oh!" said he, "there has been a great deal of exaggeration and misrepresentation about that, and I'll tell you how that was. When we got into the fort the white flag was shown at once, and the Negroes ran out down to the river; and although the flag was

JAMES GHOLSON, JR.

flying, they kept on turning back and shooting at my men, who consequently continued to fire into them crowded on the brink of the river, and they killed a good many of them in spite of my efforts and those of their officers to stop them. But there was no deliberate intention, no effort to massacre the garrison as has been so generally reported by the Northern papers."

"He said he tried to stop it; he shot his own for stealing, but he s*hot no Confederate soldier* to stop murder and massacre; liar!" said Arabelle. "Look, prisoner of war exchanges ceased around the Confederacy's refusal to exchange black prisoners of war. That's a big price to pay for refusing to exchange folks of a particular color: amazing. Stephanie Washburn, a woman, turned that up!"

"Hence Andersonville and Elmyra, with disease and horrible conditions for white soldiers on both sides," said the dean. "And there is something essentially nihilistic about having to prove racial superiority so desperately that nihilism—psychic desperation—overtakes common sense. I agree, it is amazing. Caleb, do you still have that yo-yo I gave you?"

I nodded in the affirmative. "Yessir."

"Well, son, I want to show you how to tackle that horrible nightmare that you had—the one about falling down from the Capitol Dome into the Potomac water and ice-skiing down into the mouth of a fiery dragon. Now, you had that dream after you tried to catch your keys and fell down the steps, right? At the frat house, right? And the emotions, the feeling that went along with that made you tremble in your boots, from head to toe—right?"

"Absolutely," I said, nodding after he asked, "Terror is what you felt, correct?"

"Yes," I said.

Dean said, "Always keep a toy, a drone, a squeeze ball, a yo-yo—in your pocket!"

I laughed inwardly, thinking a drone will not fit in my pocket, though I was still nodding. "When you get uptight," said the dean, "get that yo-yo—aim it uphill, any slope you think you want, any slope you want to climb, tackle, challenge, defy—and you slice it with that yo-yo, make it dance up that hill, slope, or mountain."

Arabelle was out in the hallway, cracking up. "And yo-yo 'til the cows come home. You'll feel better, you'll be less uptight, and then you can get your shoulders back into your work! Running 'round after that drone made me feel so good—ah, man, and that drone got some amazing radar images—ground penetration gets better every day!"

The dean and I had several later conversations,

but two stand out. One to mainly set a time frame for the submission of my entry to the Tennessee Office of State Parks and its Examining Board. We agreed that I would stop by for comments from a team of four professors—two from design and two from engineering—for a month, present one open session to a group of my peers, and follow up with finishing touches on the second Tuesday in October. We were set to submit when the end of October rolled around. My ideas still centered around an exedra-styled design—like Abele's at Haverford—one which reflected the very thing that our Fort Pillow forbearers *lost at close range*—in the massacre. Secesh worked to *assassinate* black Unionists' brains—*Lincoln-style*—the very thing that allowed them to *imagine* freedom! My own imagination was still working.

By mailing time, we had the imaginative architectural design twists we needed; one clue: instead of the elbow curlicues on each side of our model for the benches, we made the sides and elbow curlicues as *Segways*, in honor of Dean Davenport, and forensic science, in honor of Lara. Now the wait to hear back from Tennessee Park Service was on. And that is what we did. We waited with breath baited, yo-yos pointed uphill, fingers crossed!

XXV

To Canaan
PURITAN WAR SONG

WHERE are you going, soldiers,
With banner, gun, and sword?
We're marching South to Canaan
To battle for the Lord
What captain leads your armies
Along the rebel coasts?
The Mighty One of Israel,
His name is Lord of Hosts!
To Canaan, to Canaan
The Lord has led us forth,
To blow before the heathen walls
The trumpets of the North!

What flag is this you carry
Along the sea and shore?

JAMES GHOLSON, JR.

The same our grandsires lifted up,—
The same our fathers bore
In many a battle's tempest
It shed the crimson rain,—
What God has woven in his loom
Let no man rend in twain!
To Canaan, to Canaan
The Lord has led us forth,
To plant upon the rebel towers
The banners of the North!

What troop is this that follows,
All armed with picks and spades?
These are the swarthy bondsmen,—
The iron-skin brigades!
They'll pile up Freedom's breastwork,
They'll scoop out rebels' graves;
Who then will be their owner
And march them off for slaves?
To Canaan, to Canaan
The Lord has led us forth,
To strike upon the captive's chain
The hammers of the North!

What song is this you're singing?
The same that Israel sung
When Moses led the mighty choir,

And Miriam's timbrel rung!
To Canaan! To Canaan!
The priests and maidens cried:
To Canaan! To Canaan!
The people's voice replied.
To Canaan, to Canaan
The Lord has led us forth,
To thunder through its adder dens
The anthems of the North.

When Canaan's hosts are scattered,
And all her walls lie flat,
What follows next in order?
The Lord will see to that
We'll break the tyrant's sceptre,—
We'll build the people's throne,—
When half the world is Freedom's,
Then all the world's our own
To Canaan, to Canaan
The Lord has led us forth,
To sweep the rebel threshing-floors,
A whirlwind from the North.

Oliver Wendell Holmes